OUTWARD...
BOUND

The universe waits in perfect indifference to man. The universe has its own mysteries which it is content to contemplate. It has no need of man.

But man must press on, must challenge the universe in its frozen depths. Man explodes outward because he cannot bear the poisoned Earth that is his home. Will he become a new man out there? Will he leave behind the shackles of greed and fear that have bound his mind for all of his existence?

UNIVERSE
DAY

K. M. O'Donnell

AVON
PUBLISHERS OF
DISCUS • CAMELOT • BARD

This is the first publication of *UNIVERSE DAY*
in book form.
Some of this material has appeared in substantially
different form in: *The Magazine of Fantasy and
Science Fiction* copyright © 1969, 1970 by
Mercury Publications, Inc.
NOVA 1, © 1970 by Harry Harrison; *NOVA 2,* © 1971
by Harry Harrison *Galaxy Magazine,* © 1971 by
Universal Publishing and Distributing Corporation
INFINITY 1, © 1970 by Lancer Books, Inc.;
INFINITY 2, © 1971 by Lancer Books, Inc.

AVON BOOKS
A division of
The Hearst Corporation
959 Eighth Avenue
New York, New York 10019
Copyright © 1971 by Barry N. Malzberg.
Published by arrangement with the author.

First Avon Printing, April, 1971

AVON TRADEMARK REG. U.S. PAT. OFF. AND
FOREIGN COUNTRIES, REGISTERED TRADEMARK—
MARCA REGISTRADA, HECHO EN CHICAGO, U.S.A.

Printed in the U.S.A.

For Joyce and
Stephanie Jill Malzberg

"Here I am, 25, and still writing
Elegies for the living. You beautiful
Sonsofbitches, I know you
Walk past my walls at night, your
Shining brains turning over soundlessly,
   because
The man says 'radium' and sprays the area
With geigers before dawn. No use. You
Are my sins and you have caught up with
   me."

Trim Bissell: <u>For Friends</u>, 1968

"... I see no reason why we shouldn't go to Mars in 1982 ..."

Vice President of the U.S.
July, 1969

APOCRYPHA AS PROLOGUE OR: THE WAY WE WISH IT HAPPENED

MERCURY

Man conquered Mercury in 2119; John Golden's crew of nine fighting their way, every inch of the terrain, through Brightside, past Darkside, and into the quarters of Hut, the terrible chieftain of the Mercurian people who were, by then, a much reduced population owing to the quality of the heat which was most severe, even during the cooler periods. "We come in peace," announced Golden, as the commander of the expedition, and shot the treacherous leader through the heart. The natives were surprisingly humanoid in appearances, although they were to be distinguished by their sun-bronzed skin, the lustre of their eyes, and a curious, dull flatness to their squarish limbs which probably came from too much exercise. "I declare myself king of this here planet," Golden added to the delegation of natives assembled around their deceased chief. "I'm sorry to have used such abrupt measures but, you know, you can never tell in these highly

11

structured situations." The natives shrugged and cheered absently, a high, whistling sound coming through their ugly little nostrils. "Meni, marshik tekel upsharshin," said one of them, probably a vice-leader, and made a gesture of obeisance to the great Golden. Much moved, Golden accepted the cheers of his own men, respectfully accepted from the vice-leader what appeared to be a Mercurian version of a crown and pulled it down snugly over his ears, somewhat discomfited by a rather humid clinging which he took to be the action of a cooling device. Golden and his men reigned supreme over the planet for a period of six revolutions, after which they were instructed to return to their ship and emplane for Earth. There they were received as heroes and after many fine ticker-tape parades on the main streets of the various cities, retired into a happy and prosperous old age. The second expedition was pleased to find, when they touched Mercury six months later, that Golden was still remembered with affection and his kingly throne vacant. "Power to those who want it," the vice-leader said with that reserved mysticism which has made the remaining Mercurians so beloved to so many of us.

VENUS

Venus was conquered by man in 1993, just before the period of the Great Eastern Revolutions which held back further interplanetary adventures for some 25 years. Golin Joathan, the leader of the expedition of three; a Lieutenant Commander in the Air Force Alliance, got to the center of the Green Planet, fighting every step of the way, in an exciting adventure which may be read in transcript three rooms down the hall. There he met Horsh, head reptile of the Venusians, who were a small, decadent population living in a series of bogs in mid-planet due to the tempestuous and nearly uncontrollable spate of bad weather which had persisted on Venus since the fall of their technology. Horsh saluted Jonathan with five tentacles and said, "Welcome to this palace, we are happy to meet future denizens." Somewhat surprised at the ability of the monster to speak English, Jonathan nevertheless retained his cool-headedness and shot the beast through the center of the belly, resulting in a greenish paste being spewed over him and his men and he waited out the animal's death agony. "Oh welcome to our planet, you fair leader," another reptile, apparently a vice-lord, said and bestowed upon Jonathan the oath of office which, being rendered as it was in purest Venusian, was indecipherable. "We come in peace and jollity," said Jonathan and motioned for his men to distribute gifts; since no one in the Project had been sure of what Venusians might want or whether there even *were* any Venusians (but Congress had voted the extra appropriation just for the hell of it), they consisted of small packages of dollar bills. "Very good for exchange," winked Jonathan and reigned solemn in the bog for twelve Earth hours, but then it was time to return to the mother ship, which they did, fighting every step of the way. They were welcomed back as heroes and received ticker-tape parades on the main streets of many famous cities; then were permitted—if that is the word—to publish their memoirs, one by one, after serial rights to the official agency version had cleared. When the second expedition returned to Venus some months later, they were surprised to see that a small memorial to Jonathan still existed in the middle of a bog; it was made of stone and sinking as it was to the shoulders, yet retained a stricken grin, a frozen glare, a flicker of precision in the eyes which all agreed was exactly like the old bugger.

THE MOON

Man conquered the moon for the first time in 1969. Fighting every inch of the way, Neil Armstrong and his crew of two circled into orbit on July 19th, then landed on the satellite itself some 36 hours later. "One small step for a man, one giant leap for mankind," Armstrong said, and he and his crew-mate then proceeded to set up experiments on the moon with radioactivity, implosives and so on. Sentient life was not observed, so it was not necessary to take defensive action. After reigning over the moon for some hours, Armstrong and his companion returned to the Lunar module and then to the command ship itself, where some time later they blasted off to earth. There they were met by an enormous reception and several ticker-tape parades; afterwards they related their experiences in a book called FIRST ON THE MOON published by Little, Brown and selected as a first choice by the Literary Guild of America.

MARS

Man first conquered Mars in 1982. Fighting every inch of the way, Gull Johnson led his little expedition of two to the great Stone City on the fourth canal where were found many interesting relics of a vast Martian civilization which had apparently perished in drought many centuries ago. "We are here; we have survived, we flourish, we go on," he announced over the radio to an intercontinental hookup of several billions and then, fighting back every step of the way, the little party returned to the AMERICAN BOMBSHELL where they emplaned for Earth. There they were met by record demonstrations at the periphery of the central cities; the inner cities being occupied by riots and then received the Congressional Medal of Freedom from President Agnew. "This is a prophecy fulfilled," the President said. On nationwide television, in a joint congressional session, the three heroes then pleaded for further funding for the space program. "We must not perish on Earth," Johnson announced to enormous applause, "but must move on to the frozen spheres of Mercury, Venus and elsewhere, where we will doubtless find life and thus fulfill our destiny."

JUPITER

Jupiter was first conquered by man in 2146, shortly before the period of the Great Peril that put a halt to the great project for some 85 years. Grant John led his party of sixty-five, fighting every step of the way, through the gaseous Jovian desert and into a small amphitheatre at mid-planet where, it was rumored, the Jovians, now extinct, had held sex-festivals and lunar watches. There, John took upon himself the title of Conqueror of Jupiter, while his crew applauded, then left upon the surface of the planet a tablet of stone saying, "Here came men from Earth, Mercury, Venus and Mars, voyaging outward through the imperishable night." Fighting every step of the way, they then returned to the SUPER DESTROYER and emplaned to Earth, where they were met by a modest reception in the city, bedecked with garlands and sent through the streets of Rome on donkeys as a reconstruction, it was stated, of the coming of Christ. Afterwards, John wrote his famous novel SPEAK NOT OF EVIL, in which this and many other interesting events of his life are reported. It may be read for a small additional fee in the cubicle to the rear of the pens.

SATURN

Saturn was first conquered by man in 2231, just before the period of the Grand Plague which had such embarrassing consequences for those who caught it and turned out to be female. Fighting every step of the way, Grant Jolson and his companion traveled 650 miles in the grim Saturnian sunset to the Castle of Death, where they met the last Saturnian, a large, doglike creature who lolled uneasily on his throne. "Welcome, men of the third planet," said the evil Saturnian and expired with a shrug, popping into mist shortly thereafter and hence leaving no evidence, other than testimony, of his presence.

Next to the abandoned throne was the Saturnian's diary, which he had apparently been keeping for many centuries against Jolson's coming and since it happened, miraculously, to be written in English, Jolson was able to deduce, with the help of his skilled-linguist companion, that the coming of Earthmen to Saturn was the fulfillment of a religion which had been the center of Saturnian culture from the beginning and to which the last Saturnian had willed his own immortality to witness. "Imagine that, son of a bitch, poor old bastard, waiting all this time for us; well, at least he died happy," Jolson said and flung the diary into his satchel, winked at his companion (who was really more of a coolie, the caste system in the space program being one of the few carryovers from the less liberal traditions of history) and led him back, fighting every inch of the way, to the mother ship BOX which they rode back to Earth, being received there by a small delegation of nobles who clasped the cherished diary as it was and welcomed them back to the planet. Jolson and his companion were then executed, since it was felt that they might have too much knowledge of the customs and lore of the Fabled Saturnian Religion, whose roots and outlines had been prophesied in the new cultism of Saturniasis, originated in 2170 in the back room of a pub in Derbyshire.

URANUS

Uranus was first conquered by man in 2850, shortly after the great Final War which had devastated the planet for almost six months, ending in deadlock and vows for a lasting peace. Golden Jones, the leader of the expedition, and his 448 men, fighting every step of the way, struggled across the edge of Uranus and fell into the famous Sea of Fire, where they were all drowned except for certain artifacts which were resuscitated much later, at the time of the second expedition, in fact. The artifacts were immediately consigned to government security and may be investigated, by special permit, between the hours of 23X and 431B depending upon the authority of the visitor.

NEPTUNE

Neptune was first conquered by man in 2851. Jones Golding and his expedition of 5,000, fighting every inch of the way, came to the Palace of Crags in which a delegation of 65 Neptunians were waiting to greet them. "Oh, it is time, it is time," said one of the Neptunians, apparently the leader. "Indeed it is," said Golding and shot him through the heart with a .45 colt antique which he had retained for exactly occasions of this sort. His men proceeded then to methodically slaughter the other 64 beasts. None of their brave efforts succeeded in saving them, however, for outside the Palace of Crags, cloaked in invisibility, were several million other Neptunians who overtook the palace and slew all of Golding's men except Golding, whom they sent back to Earth with a message never to return to Neptune. Golding delivered the message, fighting every step of the way through the Government offices, and when he had delivered it to the King, fell with a pang in his heart, a Neptunian arrow, so to speak, punctured through the seat of his consciousness and with a defiant roar he expired, bringing about the famous Neptunian Revenge of 2900.

PLUTO

Man conquered Pluto in 4111. Gaul Jolding and his bird, Marsythe, fighting every step of the way, came to the center of a Plutonian desert where, it is rumored, they met God himself in the center of a shallow crevice. "Enough of this," God said, but before the villain could continue, Jolding did the necessary. He was met by a huge reception and became vice-Lord of the planet, dedicating his efforts to the conquest of the Centauris and the Foxing Of Time but unfortunately, the Grand Disasters of the Low Forties interrupted this noble program for several centuries, retarding man's progress to the stars, so that it was 6831 before man first set bomb on extra-solar territory. But that is another story entirely and of those great deeds' accounting, researchers must be referred to the other museum, three levels down and to the rear of the Slaughtering House.

I
MAKING
TITAN,
2500

NOW THERE IS NOTHING TO DO
but wait. He had plotted it out; three moons in the House
of Jupiter, a hint of tilting for chance, other manipulations;
he has taken into account the wind, the tides, the celestial
weather: now it is only a question of seeing it all proven
or, worse yet, foundering. . . . but for some reason, Kharsh
cannot sit back on it, cannot resign himself to the articula-
tion of the proven. It is a new sensation, one which he
knows he will have to meet in some intricate way back on
Earth, but for the time being he has merely integrated it
into the larger problem, the over-all set, and hoped that it
will go away. Looking through the mangled window of the
craft, seeing the slow wheel of space opening up on all
sides, speed to the left and right of him, the immensity of
that damned planet as it shows up larger and larger, no
hint of rings now, only dust, Kharsh has had to accept for
the first time what was purely unacceptable before and
that is this: *it is too large*. It is unspeakably bleak and it
encompasses. It is one thing to work this out on a zodiacal
frame, all of it abstraction, terms to be manipulated, but
another entirely to see what it looks like and he knows
that if he were not an extraordinarily strong and assured
man, he would have already given under the stress; perhaps the whole purpose of this mission—oh, the cunning
19

of that agency!—has been not so much to use as to reduce him, force Kharsh to renounce all principles of astrology at some crucial moment of connection and hurl all the charts from him in a fit of destruction, able to articulate only random lunacies about *this vastness, the vastness.* But he will not permit this to happen. He has worked too long, he has struggled too hard, the responsibility is too great. Surely, he can expect nothing from the others as well. All the more reason why he must assemble himself.

He cannot stand them. The captain has always touched off in Kharsh some vague revulsion; perhaps it has to do with the antipathy of mysticism toward natural science but more likely it is this: he has always felt inferior toward women and the captain personifies the kind of man who has always made his inner life so difficult: a big, bleakly handsome man whose very hands seem to be made for grabbing breasts and whose wife— whom he had met that once at the obligatory dinner— radiates a kind of sensuality and dependence which renders Kharsh furious, so oblivious does she seem to the tragic limitations in the captain ... limitations which Kharsh has seen from the beginning. But all the time Kharsh has been working, building himself toward this enormous moment of vindication, it is likely to assume that the captain has been screwing: he has been screwing since puberty and maybe a little before and nothing has touched him, only a crinkle of exhaustion around the eyes, perhaps a vague tremor in his voice when he talks of women, otherwise, for all the apparent difference between them, the captain would have been in isolation for decades ... and Kharsh the man tearing the bitch apart silently in bed, her eyes opening unevenly to some sense of his power. But it has not been that way at all; in the dim, noisome compact of the spaceship it would be possible to believe all differences ameliorated—nevertheless, this basic understanding persists between Kharsh and the captain and both of them know it: Kharsh has never had luck with women, the captain's has been exceptional. Or, on the other hand—and worse yet—the captain's luck has been only average and he is thus unequipped to deal with

Kharsh's envy because, in his mind, he has really accomplished so little. It is an old problem and Kharsh knows that he will have to reach a point, some time, when he will cease sentimentalizing sex but that time has not yet come. He is only 23. He needs too much, too deeply.

Rakos is another situation: what lies between him and Rakos is neither revulsion nor fear nor envy but the simple, deadly hatred of rival professionals who find their opposite views of the universe intolerable. Nothing else is of any significance although Kharsh finds a certain physical recoil has also come out of this: they are in very close quarters in the ship and he cannot stand Rakos's smell, Rakos's gestures. But these are merely symptoms: the real problem is that if Rakos has a vision of the universe which is essentially correct, then Kharsh has spent twenty years working falsehood out of a network of lies. The same is true of the captain, of course, but the captain is a simple rationalist ... the kind of man who would have been an astrologer if he had fallen into luck. Rakos, however, is in a rival specialty. He is a demonologist.

Kharsh knows that there will be no answers. They will either land on Titan and put up the flag or, like the five ships that have preceded them, sink into the ether at some anguished point and never be heard again. If they prevail, if they make this landing, it will be only because of Kharsh's careful charts and allowances, but he will always be suspect because Rakos has his pentagrams and has been conjuring flame. *He* will take the credit. On the other hand, if they perish, skidding past some coalescence of space toward gas, the captain will have to take the credit since he is only the most recent in a succession of pilots, all of whom have incurred disaster. Without the new support-team, of course. The thing, however, is that at this moment, only hours out of Titan with two weeks behind them, with this cataclysmic vindication of all that he has believed almost upon them, at this moment Kharsh is not sure that he wants to go through with it, that he wants to win through; there would somehow be more satisfaction for him if the ship were extinguished, because it would prove that although he was not right, Rakos was not right

21

either and he thinks that he may need his enemy's defeat more than his own retribution.

Omens, omens. It is difficult and complex and a sensation of winds seems to pass through the craft, winds only in his inner ear, of course, as he stumbles to his feet and hands the latest series of his charts and findings to that bastard, the captain.

REARING ABOVE HIS WIFE ON

that last night, he had held her, the captain had then had a vision: the vision was that of Titan, moon of Saturn, swimming thickly over him, his haze of desire somehow become the gaseous atmosphere of the damned planet itself and reaching for her breast, trying to move more deeply in her, he had moaned *the moon, the moon*, not knowing he was talking of the mission or only some emotional chasm within him which contained the image; no time for it either because she bucked back at him wildly, needing the fuck as much for her own sense of summation—damn her gestures!—as out of any physicality and he gave her what she needed slowly, meditatively, his orgasm more a gathering than an unfolding and fell on top of her dreamily, pinning her thickly with all his weight, thinking of Saturn's terrain and the moon from which they would have to conquer it. He had, at this moment, absolutely no fear; it was the first time in days that he had felt this way but the orgasm had drained him, left him open to vulnerability and detachment together and he knew that one way or the other he would manage the task because the two lunatics going with him on this voyage were incompetent and would be in foetal positions long, long before the moment of connection. Of this he was sure, if nothing else: he had been humiliated, made ill use of, but the final triumph would be his because demon-ologist and astrologer, both will look at him with a hushed and terrible dependence as he begins to set the control for the plunge, and even were it only to be death-and-entrapment which await them as it has been with all the others, he will have the satisfaction of knowing that of the three of them, only one will be in control. He will be in control. His wife had muttered something indistinguishable and for a moment, so deep his concentration, he thought that she had said she loved him, but she repeated it and he realized that once again she was only thinking of Rakos.

"He's crazy, he's crazy, he really wants to meet the devil," she had said, and he answered, "Only the devil in himself, the only devil that any of us can know, he turns outward the inner necessity," but this easy piece of agency-approved metaphysic did not give him the closeted sense of satisfaction it had previously, because he was slowly becoming aware for the first time of the fascination this little demonologist holds for his wife, a fascination tinged with, for all he knows, desire, and he had said, "Well, well, listen here now; it doesn't make any difference at all; out there everybody's the same, carries with him everything that he was, no changes, no changes, we are still human and nothing more," and she clasped him to her and bit his ear, saying "Yes, but I'm frightened, I'm so frightened, everybody out there is dying," and he had said, "I know. . . . but someone has to do this for the damned fools," and she said, "you'd think they'd stop; you'd think that they'd call an end to this instead of sending good men out there after the bad, particularly you."

And he had said then—what the hell was he talking about, anyway?—"but we need this moon. We need it very badly, the space of it; it gives us a position straight down to Saturn you see, we've got to have the planets because we've got no room anymore, nothing contains us. We've got to move out."

"But nobody's living on any of the planets! No one ever will!"

"Ah," he had said, "that's the point, we've got to find a planet that we can live on so we can go there and Saturn's next. Jupiter was close but no good, Mars was dead, Venus we can't even talk about, it's all been a swindle so far but we're still trying. We'll always try. They need it too bad, you see, they can't give it up."

23

"You want to go," she had said in a flat voice, pointed a finger on his chest and pressed down. "That's all. You really want to go. You can't even admit it but you want to be out there."

"Yes," he had said, "that's true all right. I want to go out there, I want to make this space and land on Titan because we've got to make it and we have got to prove that there is nothing up there that we do not understand; it is all coming clear, merely that we must extend what we know to encompass it," and he had thought then that he had never said it so well and had never been more aware of why Rakos, that madman, and Kharsh, the little astrologer, must hate him. Rationality and mysticism; the devil and physics, the crumbling void and the maps of space: this was the basic opposition and there could be only one answer, although the fact that most men would dedicate their lives to circumvention had always filled him with a high and solemn terror. But he does not want to get any further into it, not then, not now; no, he is in too deep already and so he had only returned to his wife's breast, squeezing the nipple, making it form a small pinnacle, attacking that pinnacle as if it were Titan itself and he could cleave out that satellite as easily as he could make her thrash against him in her slow-building response to the only manipulations he has ever truly understood ... or trusted. "You're hurting me, you're hurting me," she had cried but far gone into it, drifting deep into the painless torment, he had held her in a grasp so firm that her breasts had felt like metal beneath him, grinding absently through his palms.

RAKOS DRAWS THE PENTRAM

with a flourish and then steps back a few feet, as much space as he can give it, checks the thing from all angles and then moves in to color the edges with chalk. Now that he has come so near the culmination, he finds that his heart is beating rapidly, his respiration seems sweaty and unpleasant, but this means far less to him than the necessity to get it right because once the process has begun there will certainly be no reversal and a misplaced angle, any slight alteration from the structural formula, and the devil will leap from the center and devour all of them. In a sense, Rakos finds himself thrilled by this; it would be a satisfactory vindication of everything he has believed and would, in the bargain, have an effect on the captain so spectacular that none of them, listening at home, would be able to doubt what he has done . . . but Rakos still thinks that he thinks too well of himself to look for triumph in disaster. Besides, the devil is the only way out of this and he knows that he will do their bidding, for vanity's reasons, if none other. The pentagram goes swiftly now that he has established the basic design and when he steps back a second time, he knows that there is nothing more he can do. In due course he will chant the spells and summon the devil and then they will see what happens.

He hates Kharsh.

He thinks of his hatred.

He wishes that there was some way in which he would communicate to Kharsh not only the full fact of his revulsion but the *reasons* for it: the fact is that Kharsh is only codifying the captain's idiocies in another fashion and there is no difference between them. Kharsh, no less than the captain and the system that has sent them there, believes in charts, believes in cause-and-effect, believes in rational principles to underlie all disasters and succeeds, but in his case his rationalism has been transmogrified into a crank's stupor. Only cranks or failed saints would go into astrology in the first place; it is merely a bastardization of science without its rigor but with the same old shibboleths. There must be some way, Rakos has often reflected, that he can make clear to the captain that he and Rakos have more in common than Rakos and Kharsh; that Kharsh is merely another version of the damned scientists who have sent them into dying voyage. But to the captain this would be deep reasoning, it would be impossible for this simple man to pursue the chain since he feels himself hounded by lunatics on left and right and there would be no way of convincing him that Rakos is the salvation while Kharsh only sinks into the stupefied fear that all of the others must have felt when their ships disappeared into the rings. Rakos has tried to have nothing to do with Kharsh during this voyage but the quarters are small and occasionally they have been forced to exchange words. Fortunately, he is the only one of them permitted to work in the single small room off the main cabin; he has made it known long in advance that spells must be cast in privacy. (This is not strictly true but in many ways comes close to the point; the devil will obey the one who raised him and a multiplicity of personalities means the possibility of conflicting orders.) This and this alone has perhaps moved him from hounding madness and, possibly, a violent attack upon Kharsh.

He is ready, now, to summon the devil and can do it at any time now, but at this crucial instant he hesitates. They are still an hour or so away from entry fire and as long as the devil is summoned any time before this, he will accomplish their salvation; in the meantime, he does not want to waste time with extraneous dialogue. At least this is what Rakos tells himself; inside he is honest and rational enough to admit that it is probably something else holding him back in the name of simple fear, something far more complex. He has, after all, never summoned the devil before. He has dreamt of him behind a thousand closed doors, has embraced him through a hundred nights, has seen his effigy swung enormous above shouting crowds, has judged his effect upon people in whom he dwelt, his work in the heavens themselves . . . but he has never spoken with or met him and he does not know, at this moment, if he is ready to do it. It is not scruple. This is not the issue, it is something else entirely. In the first place, he is not exactly sure what he will want to say to him.

Granted that the devil has a certain limited omnipotence, he may be spared the exposition of course: as a matter of fact, he has counted on this because it would take him entirely too long to bring the devil up to date otherwise. How would he do it anyway? *Well, to begin with, they've lost six ships attempting to negotiate a land-*

ing on Titan, now the government has soured on physics and has decided to try it our way; I'd appreciate you giving us a very soft landing and if you could do something about that bastard Kharsh while you're at it, nothing serious, just a minor embolism or the like that would keep him out of action until we returned, I'd really appreciate it. Would that be the way? But that would hardly move into the sheer complexity of the matter or make it understood that there is, in effect, no government any more but only this single and enormous agency whose powers of decision are little more than reflex and which can be cleverly manipulated in almost any fashion. *We need your assistance in making a landing on Titan, sir; our instruments seem to have failed us?* That would hardly offer the devil any inducement for his good works. No, there has to be a simple, cause-and-effect relationship established here; a promissory arrangement, as it were, but what has come upon Rakos slowly and with building intensity in these last hours is a question of simple puzzlement: he has not the faintest idea of what offer the devil might take. To summon him is one thing and he has never doubted that he could do it. To negotiate is another. He has no bargaining position. Furthermore, it would be in the devil's rather perilous nature to let them plunge into emptiness as have all the others; he can hardly, after all, appeal to the devil's better nature. Not on any simple level, at any rate.

Rakos is confused. He is not even sure of what he is going to do. He kneels at last before the pentagram, tailor fashion, elbows hooked around his knees and for a long, whirling time, he looks on it while all of his history seems to overtake him until there is nothing but the pentagram before and emptiness behind and somewhere in between these two he knows he will have to piece out a judgment so momentous as to partake of the very wheel-and-splice of the universe itself, but there is simply no space, no space whatsoever in which to work it out, and he does not know if the lack is within himself or merely some anticipatory whiff of the devil's conundrum, waiting thickly for him in hell until the proper time. *You don't really want to get down on Titan, do you?* the devil will ask with an

27

engaging grin. Along about now, after all, you should be thinking of what you may find there. Or maybe you don't care, is that it? If so, my crankiest and most lecherous demon has absolutely nothing on you.

NOW HE MUST TALK TO THE

captain; there is no way about it. Kharsh staggers from his bunk, enfolds the charts in his arms and stumbles toward the forward part of the main cabin where the captain sits, facing space, making computations on a sheet of archaic paper, feeding tape into the computer. "Look here," Kharsh says, "come on now. We've got to do some talking about this now. We can't put it off any more, don't you see that?"

"I can't talk," the captain says. "I'm preparing for the landing. Can't you see that I'm busy, you idiot? There's no time. There's no time for anything."

"But there are certain things which must be taken into account, beginning now. Calculations! Now, in the first place, the three moons—"

"I can't listen to that crap, don't you understand me!" the captain screams and throws back a hand. His intention must have been only to dramatize his fear, but what happens is that he hits the charts, which scatter with a hiss all through the cabin, then settle windlessly to the floor. "I warned you," the captain is saying, looking at his fist. "I warned you. I didn't want to do it. Why did you make do this? Don't you have any reserve?"

"Now," Kharsh says, and finds that he too is shouting, "now it's too late; it is too late for all of you, by the time I get these things back in order we'll be wiped out. Do you want to die? Do you *want* death, you son of a bitch?" He can not remember having cursed before. Perhaps it has only had to do with leading a relatively sheltered existence.

"Listen," the captain says and turns full on him for the first time; it is as if, Kharsh feels, they have never truly looked upon one another before and now, long past the point of possible contact, they have stripped one another bare. "Listen, you old charlatan you, you thief, you idiot: I didn't ask for either of you fuckers to be put on this craft and I don't have to listen to you. I'll make the maneuvers. I'll make the landing. You and Rakos stay in the other cabin and *keep the door shut* and don't make a sound or come out until we're done. If you don't do that, I'll kill you. I mean it. I won't put up with it any more. There are limits to what a man should take."

And in that instant, then, Kharsh sees all of it; the fullest implications, the total meaning of what not only he but all of the predecessors have been through, the reasons why they have been put on the craft, the reason that he went into astrology, the reason, even, that Rakos fell into demons; he sees all of this and more, but it is too much for him, entirely too much, because nothing in or out of his science has equipped him to deal with it, *we must stop misdirecting,* he thinks wildly. "You want to die," he says, "just like all the others you see. You want to die. You'd rather die than admit you can't deal with it, that's the whole of it. That's why the program collapsed five times already and had to be started all over again. Because it was run by men like you. And it's only going to be this way, as long as you're around."

"I'm going to make the landing," the captain says, "and after I've made it, I'll deal with you. I'll deal with you both. Now get away from me or I'll kill you." He draws a pistol, levels it on Kharsh, closes his eyes in some trauma of concentration which Kharsh knows could be the last thing he will ever see unless he withdraws. "I won't put up with it," the captain says. "You see, I just can't take this any more."

And Kharsh withdraws. He has no alternative, he wants to live, in or out of the Rising Moons. Now his charts are lying through the cabin, crinkling, smudged, on the verge of desiccation ... but he does not stop to retrieve them. He does not go to Rakos either. Instead, he returns to his bunk and, straddling it, eyes toward the ceiling, seeing the flatness, the faint overhanging mist in the atmosphere, knowing that this will be the last thing that he will ever see and all for the better, all for the better, because his life has been a misdirection and he did not go into astrology for the right reasons after all, but only to flee the men with dull eyes who tried to make the landings. That was the reason. That was what drove him there. That and no success with women. He cannot bear to touch it.

RISING FROM HIS WIFE ON THE

last morning, the captain had washed and dressed quickly, trying not to look at her, trying to be in all but the physical sense already somewhere else, but at breakfast he could not continue this and at a glance found her against his chest sobbing, brushing her hair back from the eyes, clutching him. "I'm frightened," she had said, "I'm just so terribly, terribly frightened: it's all gone crazy, hasn't it now?" and he was able to only nod slowly, a stricken yank of his head in accord because it was true and, in the bargain, he had only wanted to pacify her, "we've gone back to barbarism," he had said, "you see, it's all a question of lapsed technology, we really haven't been able to live with it as long as it's been around; now the soothsayers point out ways among the deadly machines, only they too say they see the light. But we need Titan," he had added, "we need Titan, we need this space, we've got to keep on going out even though it's all failed so far, everything, only the damned ships work, not the men any more, but we've got to try," and he had realized that he had summed it up for her then as well as he was apt to sum up this thing for the rest of his life, and it was too much to undertake, certainly these speculations on top of his fear were entirely too much and so, clutching over the breakfast table, he had tried then to fuck her, fuck her into either silence or submission, but he got neither. It didn't work. She had been cooperative, eagerly so, had lunged open under him and he had pursued her to the floor, but she had been dry and full of conversation and only his own efforts had distracted him, a sick withered thrashing with nothing at the end but distention, gloom, pain and so he had finally removed himself and had stood, had said, "I think we've got to come to the end of this thing now; you'll hear from me all the way, we'll be in radio contact and I'll be back and everything this time will be fine."

"What about the others?" she had said then, during the fucking she had said, *I bet Rakos fucks like the devil* and *make believe you're a spaceship and I'm Titan,* but now strictly business again, "the five others that didn't do so fine," and there it was between them finally and she said, "I think you want to die; I think you want to make an end of yourself. All of you do, you're committed to death, you want to sleep with it, it's the only thing you think you understand."

"Don't worry," he had said, "we've got a horoscope and demon-slayer on board, so we know they'll let us through the gates," and then they had begun to laugh, laugh and laugh with sick, wrenching cries, and as for the rest of it: how the hell he had gotten out of that house, what he had said to her, what pact they had made, what got him to the base itself, he had no idea. It was only a grey, dim space in which, like fish, qualities like dread, hope, pain and terror swam absently, and if he could ever catch those fish he would find their dull faces a mirror of his own: blind eyes gaping toward the starless night.

RAKOS HEARS THE SOUNDS FROM

the cabin, understands what is going on. . . . but does not intervene. There is nothing that he can do. What these two now understand about one another and themselves, he knew from the beginning. *No.* No, he is far beyond all this nonsense, out in some cove of his own, upon him and no one else rest the responsibilities for landing the mission safely and now, locked into their postures, the other two must not interfere. It is time to raise the devil and to consult with him. It is time to make the pact that will land them on Titan and open a new era of exploration and progress, safety and expansion, the devil and man hand in hand against the void. For thousands of years it has been driving toward this conclusion: only scatology and damnation can know the stars. But he cannot do it. He cannot make his body move from the bunk.

He cannot raise the devil.

He does not want to summon him and at the realization of what he has been so simply putting beyond himself all these years he feels himself shudder, then assimilates it and moves on to a newer level of thought. For all of his life, Rakos now understands, he has not wanted to raise the devil so much as himself ... and now, at the moment of confrontation, he cannot go through with it, cannot truly come to terms with the understanding that from the spaces of the pentagram may vault not so much the devil as some vision of Rakos himself, bloated, eyes staring, mouth raving, hands clutching: yes, he would not have understood how much cunning and pain there had been in him, how much displacement, but now, working out in the far spaces, disconnected as he has never been, he is willing to make this admission.

He is willing to make a list of admissions. What has happened to him here, why is it so clearly upon him? Demonology may be a legitimate science or at least an art but it was not legitimacy that drove him there but something else . . . something which he cannot accept. The devil may or may not come out of the pentagram but Rakos must be mute. He can ask him no favors. For the devil . . . well, the devil owes him nothing.

Nothing, nothing at all: all the obligations work the other way because the devil, or at least his image, has propped him up, kept him going lo! these many years and now there is only framework. He feels a whirling in the ship, a hint of dislocation, and understands that they are going down, there is a shaking wrench and he understands further that the same thing is about to happen to them as has happened to the five other ships and that they will never be seen again. Perhaps it is death that is overtaking him but it does not feel like death, it is some other quality, something which he cannot name but he knows the devil would understand, would be able to label for him

32

if they could speak. Too late he resolves to do it anyway, raise up Lucifer and have a finish to it, but before he can move from the bunk, something like a fist hits him in the center of the stomach and his nerves gather around to encircle it, bring it into his being; then there is only sobbing, gasping, wrenching and pain and at the last moment, then, Rakos understands almost everything but it is far too late of course to tell the others. It is far too early to make any use of it himself. They are primitives. They cannot deal with it.

II
SOME HEADLINES IN THE VOID
1968

A SPECULATION: THE EARTH

Miller floats slowly, revolving head to heels, pulling up his T-shirt to show the outlines of his stomach. "Lice," he says. Thomas tells him to cut it out. I am working on the charts during this and therefore have no time to get between them, no interest either, but I can sense their hatred. It is cold inside this capsule and soon enough Miller replaces his clothing and his suit while Thomas efficiently checks out the equipment.

INTIMATIONS FROM DEAD-CENTER

Miller says that if the retro-rocket refuses to fire, he will spend the last days of his life telling everybody down on earth exactly what he thinks of them. "Remember," he reminds us, "radio transmissions will be unaffected. *Completely unaffected.* I intend to start at the beginning of my life and not stop until the present and all along the way I will make very clear that I know what they have done to me. Down to the last detail. I will give them a sense of communal guilt that will take them seventy years to outlive, forget about the assassinations. I will personally tie up this project until the end of the century by destroying public opinion. I find being a potential sacrifice unpleasant, you see. I don't mind the procedure but I don't have to *perform* for them." Thomas points out that all of the tests indicate that the rocket will fire perfectly; if not, this was something of which we were all well aware before the flight and we had offered to take the risks anyway. It is contractual. He reminds Miller as well that he is the commander and can bar this kind of demonstration. To all of this—Thomas is only trying to do his job—Miller laughs. "We'll have the television on," he says. "I'll point out a few things to them on the way. I'll show them I have a prick. Bet you fifty cents half of them down there don't think we've got them."

A RETROSPECTION

Control has reminded us to avoid obscenities conscientiously along with the double-entendres while on the network and to stay properly dressed and disciplined during the television interludes. It has been made clear to us that we must do nothing to offend the huge audience which comes along with us; furthermore, misbehavior can set the project back irrevocably. Thomas has assented to this with enthusiasm and has dedicated himself to enforcing tight discipline in the capsule, but Miller says that he is only waiting until the time when the retro-rockets fail, then he will do the necessary. Or what he deems to be the necessary. "We cannot live our lives as if the bottom two-thirds of them do not exist," he has said. "If we go out into space we carry the best and the worst of us all

35

bound up together and we should not behave otherwise." I find the instructions from control extremely irritating too, of course, but they have precedent: no one, to the best of our knowledge, has ever uttered a curse while on open communication from space. There are rumors that during one of the first expeditions, one member of the crew, who will be known as X, was refused permission to join the others on transmission because he had previously threatened to wish his wife a happy birthday in a most entirely graphic manner. Of course, X later said that he had only been playing and that there had been no right in denying him greetings from space, but the commander on that voyage had not thought the chance worth taking.

It is not that space is aseptic—and here I am cribbing from Miller—so much as the impression is given that we should be on our best behavior.

BEING ON MY BEST BEHAVIOR

We defecate and urinate inside our spacesuits: plumbing would be impossible at this primitive stage of the project and, similarly, the idea of placing receptacles around the craft was vetoed at a responsible level early in the project: the resulting mess would leave a very bad impression for the recovery crews although, of course, sealed inside our masks for the most part, we would be oblivious to it. At those times that we remove our masks, the odor might remind us of our origins. Nevertheless, the rules on elimination are very strict and we are careful to void just before the television transmissions so that by no unnatural wink or glimmer of eye will we rivet audience attention to the suspicion of scatology in the void.

AN IMPRESSION OF THE VASTNESS

Looking out the window, through the haze and ice, we can glimpse the slow spin of the universe itself, working back against the frozen earth and moon which from this angle are stationary and pinned against what seems to be an enormous, toneless tent. Vague flickers of light seem to move in the distance but the stars are no brighter than on a cloudy night at home; perhaps we have a bad vantage point ... or, perhaps, the illusion of the brightness of these stars is just that, poet's junk. Most of the time we try not to look out, although control, of course, is very interested in our impressions. Of particular interest are the comments Thomas raises on the appearance of the earth, its greenness, its homogenous tranquillity when seen from this enormous height. "It seems impossible to imagine how there can be war or strife; it seems impossible to imagine war or strife; it seems impossible to imagine how the children of mankind cannot live together in peace and harmony, faced with the awfulness of space," Thomas says, and control asks him to repeat that: the transmission seems a bit unclear.

THOMAS SPECULATES ON OUR DESTINY

Away from the responsibility of the transmissions, not involved with challenging Miller, Thomas proves to be an entertaining, relaxed man, full of the responsibility of being the commander, but at the same time possessing that kind of humorous detachment which probably underlies his seniority. Surprisingly, I never got to know him very well at base; we are separated by ten years chronologically and Thomas says that there is no way our generations can understand one another. Nevertheless, once the final flight plans were drawn and he came to understand that both Miller—whom he really dislikes—and I would be accompanying him, he did everything within his power to establish a cordial relationship, including Miller and myself being invited over to dinner several times with his family, a dull, strapping group of people whose names, numbers and rank I have never been quite able to catch. Since Miller and I were not/and never have been married or even keeping serious company, we were unable to reciprocate in that way. Now, in the capsule itself, Miller and Thomas rarely speak to one another except during the broadcasts when a certain forced amiability must prevail, otherwise they can get at one another only through me, Miller because he feels that by being his age I am an ally, Thomas because I have never made the kind of melodramatic threats which Miller has. Resultantly, Thomas must rely upon me for conversation and since there is plenty of time for that—our tasks, despite all the publicity, are really quite minimal—I have gotten to know a good deal about him over the past few days; he believes that the importance of our mission is overrated because it really has nothing to do with solving the problems back on earth and yet, at the same time, he says he understands that the project is meeting needs for people which nothing there will allow. "This is why I don't permit any cursing on the broadcast, you see," he says, "aside from anything which control would order. We have to make a fresh start; we can't carry on and on this way, always and forever," giving Miller a sidewise look. "X was a nice fellow but he thought that the whole thing was a game, a power game, an adventure game, and that was why he got himself grounded; not only because of the dirty jokes. If it were up to people like X, we would inhabit all the places of the galaxy and all of them would turn out like this one: the same poison, the same corruption. I don't believe that we were born having to be this way; we just kind of evolved. There can be a counter-solution in space."

Miller, hearing all of this—there is no way, after all, he can avoid it—turns to ask if what Thomas really has on his mind is the banning of sex in space in addition to any scatological references. "You know what I meant," Thomas says angrily. "Well," Miller replies, "the three of us can't have sex together, not with these gadgets switching us into control any time at all and without warning, so that means we have a flying start. Isn't that right?" and I have to make some remark about course corrections in order to stave off the tension.

ALL IS NOT ADVENTURE: WE SLEEP

In the slow, turning night of the capsule, heavy and gasping under the load of seconal they have insisted we all take, I can hear beyond Thomas's slow, even breath at the watch the quicker, higher gasps coming over the radio; it is as if lying in this entrapment, I were not alone but being surveyed by millions of eyes, all of the eyes frantic and burning, sunk in their isolation, trying to get a grip on me through the television receiver, trying to understand through the web of my sleep what separates my darkness in space from theirs on earth. It is an uncomfortable sensation to know what we are carrying on this voyage and so I must spend the majority of my supposed sleep-time trying to count off the minutes and, for comfort, imagining that I am lying on a closely enclosed field, surrounded by sheep.

MILLER'S VISION OF THE FUTURE

"As far as I can see, within fifty years, we'll have such misery and congestion on earth as cannot be dreamt of now; such corruption and breakdown as to stagger the soul and then, spread out on the thin aseptic boards of the planets and their satellites will be small colonies populated by people like Thomas, living in shells at a cost of one million dollars per square inch of gravity. And they'll be in constant contact with the earth on a network of fourteen new television channels set up to receive each of the colonies and in every bar room, in every living room throughout the nation, will be a group of people sweltering in darkness, watching what is coming through on those sets and dreaming of a better end for themselves.

"And then there will be the riots, too, terrible riots when they get hold of the transmitters in the projects and try to cancel the whole thing out, kill the personnel, but they'll always be stopped because the most real thing, the most important thing, will be what is going on in those colonies and the government will do anything—*anything* to keep it coming in.

"And the worst part of it is that they'll live on Ganymede or Jupiter, just about the way regressed patients live in a clean mental hsopital: plenty of paint and projects and no connection at all. So that's what's coming, what they will beam in will be worthless. That's what I can't stand. I can't stand to talk about any of this any more right now."

MY VISION OF THE FUTURE

I am not so sure that Miller is correct: in the first place, he is able to assume a continuing order of technology which will permit the extension of the space program along the lines we have started. I foresee, rather, lapses: fitful, if not complete, social and technological reversals which will force us to begin again in space every two centuries or so, largely to the same purposes, because there is no way in which we will ever discover how to make use of it. But of those thoughts I try to take little heed, they do not fit my function, would be disliked by the project, and in any event do not connect with the particular *corporeality* of the situation here. For all the distance, we have never been so inside ourselves.

THE MOMENT OF CONNECTION

After we settle into orbit, Thomas reminds us that transmission will begin in fifteen minutes. We start the cameras clicking off their pictures of the moon and Miller puts his helmet back on. I can see Thomas working on his suit with a rag which he has appropriated from some place; into the rag pour the grease and rust which the rays of space have pocketed on him like an artifact.

THE ATTEMPT TO BREAK FREE

The retro-rockets fire immediately and we can feel the power drive us back against the seats; Thomas half rises from his own chair and takes off his helmet.

"See, I told you," he says, "there was never any problem at all. The whole danger was concocted by control, just as a means of keeping interest. 'Give them a little peril, it never hurts,' you know. Without danger there's no fun. No fun for us, either. Give them their bread and circuses, you see." But his voice is shaking and we can see that Thomas too had questioned; if what he says is true, then it would have been even more logical for control to have arranged for us to stay there forever, a beacon and a monument, a symbol of the pride and death intermingled, which are all we can know of space. Miller too must understand this because he says nothing.

"Well?" Thomas says to him. "Are you sorry that you lost your opportunity? It would have been a great thing, really a wonderful performance for you. And I wouldn't have even tried to stop you. How's that for my secret?"

"I know you wouldn't have," Miller says, "but I have a secret too. My secret is that I really wouldn't have done it. I would have been too scared, I would have fallen apart under stress. Only the really strong can do the things that they must die to do and I am not that strong. But you are, Thomas. You would have done it. And now you know everything."

I see then, in their laughter, that we have not been so far apart during this voyage, after all; the distance was

only a state of consciousness, not the terrible drifting quarter of a million miles that we must yet go to return—
  Well, to return to what?

III
TRACKING THE MOONS OF MARS 2042

DEIMOS

He sees it as if from a great distance but it is really close, close onto him the bugger, the shallow surfaces of that sphere no more than three or four miles dead ahead. It looks like machinery. All of it is machinery; he has consoled himself into remembering that: the satellites, the planet, the ship that takes them there, his own wicker and sniff of blood is nothing but a question of engineering and so he invokes this knowledge against the more ancient dreads which pursue him, trying to stifle the mad, merry monologue which has assaulted him on this mission: WE DO NOT BELONG HERE, WE HAVE NO BUSINESS HERE, WE ARE TRESPASSING ON SOME UNITY WE DO NOT UNDERSTAND. WE DO NOT UNDERSTAND/THE VERY LAND/WHICH WE WALKED ON EARTH/THAT STRICKEN TURF/OH WHERE OH WHERE IS THE ALIEN GONE, he sings, conscious of the fact that he is probably going insane, but this, after all, is only a natural phenomenon, a con-

43

comitant, as it were, of the great ride itself. OH YOU BUGGERS, OH YOU MUGGERS, WE'LL FIND AND DESTROY YOU FOR OUR FREE EARTH, he mutters and cuts out the drive, cuts all power in the void, lets himself drift into some kind of stationary orbit looking down (or is it merely up?) at that damned moon, trying to reconcile himself to the feelings that he knows will surely come: awe, mystification, wonder, fear, curiosity, etc., etc., etc. But there are no such feelings at all, only a kind of vague dismay which is instantly subsumed in its more technological overlay, and he remembers what he is there to do: he is to take findings, try to ascertain whether Deimos might at some time in the past have been able to shelter sentient life; was not, in fact, put up for that purpose so that the aliens could use it as a tracking-station. The important thing, he understands, is to get hold of the sources of the aliens so that they can trace it back . . . and kill all of them. That part makes sense. He will do, then, certain mappings and adjustments which will lead the project yet one more transient—but vital, vital, everything was vital—step and so he does this, going to his pocket computer and graphs, letting the technology take over for him. Now there is no singing. He does not even recollect what he was singing about. Perhaps it was only some refraction of a popular tune he learned on earth, the leading hit in recent months and therefore only a nervous reflex, nothing more. OH, WE CAN CONQUER THE FULLNESS OF SPACE/BUT NOT THE INWARD DEPTHS/FOR THAT, FOR THAT CAN ONLY BE DONE/BY YOO-HOO-HOO-HOO-HOO he mutters, while the machinery titters and squeaks in the background and the slow, guiding huff of the sensors assesses all that has to be known of Deimos, robot moon of Mars.

PHOBOS

In the tracking device she has picked it up clearly now, moving its wavering way across the path of the heavens, stars strewn to the back of it; the front, the left and right. *Oh it's beautiful, beautiful to behold,* she murmurs, trying to construct some kind of poem which will both show her appreciation of the moment and communicate to the others, later, what it all means on some near-metaphysical level. *Passenger of the night/Child of the Unborn/Scepter of the Red Planet!* she will get all of this down on her typewriter as soon as she is relieved and send it to the quarterlies, the moment she returns to Mars. In the meantime, however, there is very little to do but to relax and let the instruments perform their work: they have Phobos on a dead-set and in due course will tell her everything she needs to know about the dimensions of its orbit, the characteristics of its mode. She struggles against the renewed realization that she is nothing but a functionary and that this machinery works in such a fashion as to make her presence only audacious, certainly irrelevant, and then finally gives up, mutters the hell with it, allows the speculations to come and go. Gloomy they are; fine and gloomy, there is poetry in them, to say nothing of various levels of apperception, and she knows that whatever else she has been well served by her time on this project cause, when she returns she will no longer be a technician on an aimless project, but a poetess. Somewhere she has read that it is Deimos, the other one, which is the artificial satellite, Phobos the natural, but why anyone would have wanted to construct a satellite for this damned planet is beyond her. It is difficult in any case to keep hold of all this; it is not her specialty, nothing except the mathematics is her specialty and it is dull and depressing anyway because the origin of the satellites has nothing to do now with her condition or her ambitions; in any event, they are only meaningful as they relate to her own inner terrain, her own inner space as it were and the rest of the project, the entire governmental swindle that sent them up here can only be a kind of unwitting sanctification of that knowledge. Once some boy —she forgets exactly which one—had swung over her and in the heat of necessity had made a fast penetration-and-orgasm in total, stunned silence, all of this so rapid that

45

his semen felt in her as the cold sweat does now, a slight trickle both centrifugal and peripheral to her purposes, a pulse of irrelevance in the bending night; yes, that too, she thinks and reminds herself that she will have to include this image in the poem she will be writing. She has no fear now; the CAROLINA REVIEW or *Knife!* certainly cannot reject her any more, she will be the only lady poet who has gone to Mars; there will even be the possibility of an anthology or a grant or two, and at the thought of how far she has had to go to make some minuscule connection between the layers of self, she smiles and quickens while Phobos swims slowly dreaming across the channel of light and the stars themselves, nothing but a blanket, seem to swaddle upon her.

MARS

Therefore, you must understand that there is some basic misapprehension here, the whole purpose of the survey is nullified because the premises were wrong and, hence, we will find nothing, he writes, but it is the tenth time that he has tried this approach and he is not satisfied, not satisfied at all, in fact, he is disgusted because there is no way that he can seemingly impress upon the bureaucracy either by code or wire the true horror of what is happening here. *Gentlemen, we retain our humanity always,* he has written, and *the further we go the more limited we become; it is the only just compensation for fear of endless frozen spaces* and this had been a good beginning, he had been pleased with it, almost moved, but now he has no way of knowing how to proceed and he knows, furthermore, that if he sends this kind of wire, his career will be finished. They will not even allow him to participate with the rest of the group in the parades, the luncheons, the Congressional ceremonies and the rest of it; that is how isolated he will become. Nevertheless, he must struggle with it: the intimation has come upon him in these last days that he is dealing with a situation so momentous and final by turns that if he does not take the responsibility for its explication, no one ever will. Besides, he is the Commander. *You must be made aware of this delimitation; the further we go, the less we are,* he continues, *and in any event the terrain here is no more intrinsically dismaying than the far Antarctic, it must be other things, other considerations which are driving all of us quite mad. You must, gentlemen, be prepared to embrace some kind of metaphysic if you wish to continue,* and then, with a flare of revulsion, he picks up everything he has written and throws it into his wastebasket because it is no good, he knows that now, there is no way that he can possibly make it clear to them: the whole thing has been mad and nothing madder but the voyage itself which shakes slowly toward disaster on the shoulders of the fifteen men and five women who have been sent there. *Inner space is outer space is middle earth and we've no birth* he hums, one of the popular hits when the expedition left earth and he reflects that in the popular culture, anyway, the more complex things have appeared, the more simple they have been made. He feels a trembling in his shoulder blades or is it merely an itch, a difficult discrimination to make and then palpates a hand against his forehead. Yes, he has a fever. Moving from the bunk, moving from the room, seeking the medic for a diagnosis, he is unaware of the man tracking Deimos, the woman tracking Phobos, but this will end, this too will end, everything will come together in the long or short run of it and of this he would, in any case, have been convinced: they have plans for him and have always had them, only the enactment remains unsure.

IV

OFFERTORY & RESOLUTION

In that night, the fifteenth since his return, the astronaut dreams for the first time and in this dream he is campaigning for public office. Down the main street of the town in which he was born he parades. Beside him is the state chairman of his party and on the other side his wife but he is only dimly conscious of them, his wife in particular, being, he feels, linked instead to the crowd which is curiously mobile for all its size. The crowd pursues him down the tunnel of the street so that the parade is not seen in so much a succession of faces but the same, coming after him with ever greater speed as the big convertible accelerates. The strain of running seems to afflict some of the older members of the crowd with seizures. Their faces stretch in pain but they love him and will not stop.

"Wonderful, wonderful!" the state chairman is saying, "there's never been anything quite like this before," and the astronaut turns to him to learn exactly what it means—but before he can the scene dissolves and many hands seem to pull him from the car. Now he is on a handshaking tour of the business district. Waves of people assault him with their thumbs and as he touches each of them they crumple and seem to gasp. "You were beautiful on the Moon," a woman says, "you were just so beautiful, dancing like a big bear on those funny rocks."

"Thank you," the astronaut says, "I will appreciate your vote."

"How was it planned?" she asks, "I mean the choreography, who worked that out?" and he says "it wasn't a show, ma'am, I mean, we had certain policies and procedures, that was all."

"Oh nonsense," she says with a wink, "the whole thing was just wonderful, we all loved it where we were and you haven't got a thing to worry about." She is a rather pretty, distracted woman wearing a sleeveless dress in a print made of rocketships and he is just at the point of telling her that the name of their spaceship is misspelled when the state chairman appears and lifts him high to a platform, introducing him as the favorite son of the state. "Mighty pleased, mighty pleased for all of us here," the chairman says and the square turns into a banquet hall and the crowd into dinner guests and the astronaut understands now that this is a fund-raising dinner and he must give a speech.

Despite the fact that with the exception of the transmissions and the press conference, he has never given a public appeal in his life, he finds himself surprisingly at ease. "I'm very pleased, mighty pleased to be here," he says. "You understand of course that the whole thing was a group effort. Individual pyrotechnics and heroism are meaningless in the lunar age. The individual must be measured in terms of the contribution he can make to the whole," and looks for his wife. She is by his side, crouching on her chair to give an illusion of height (she is quite a small woman, really) eying him with bemusement and he puts his hand on the strange softness of her hair saying, "she was the one who made me stay with the program anyway. If it weren't for her I would have quit years ago because I thought that it was all too mechanical, dreadful machines I mean to say, but this lovely woman made me see the beauty of it," and the crowd applauds. "As far as my program," he says after counting twenty, "as far as that I think that the state has to look forward rather than behind, the lunar age means greater responsibilities and those responsibilities must fall to the kind of men who have learned to cooperate with one another in the post-technological era." The state chairman, who has handed him the text of this speech sometime earlier (perhaps it was in the car) leads the heavy applause and then he leaves the podium, returning to his dinner which he finds has now been totally consumed by his seven-year-old son who was smuggled into the banquet under a waiter's coat and now has become some kind of a grotesque alien, growling over the food.

Now he dreams that it is some hours after the banquet. He is holding his wife in the hotel room and saying, "I don't know, I mean I just don't know if I really want this. It has to be done I suppose but I had thought of something somehow a little less *public,*" and she says flatly, "listen darling, you were on your way out of this program anyway, you know the pressures that the liberals were building up and that psychological stuff you were covering and now you might as well put all that bullshit to *some* use." The astronaut comes to understand with some pain that he had lied during his after-dinner speech, the argument had run in exactly the opposite way . . . and his wife has always hated the program. He decides to fuck her—

but moving over her, rearing, bucking, he connects to some sense of himself in the gloom of her cunt only to find that his orgasm is a whimper and he falls from her quite lost, quite spent. "I just don't know," he says. "I just don't know. It all seems so pointless somehow, even though it's for the good of the nation."

He dreams then that he is at the state convention accepting the official nomination of his party and as he moves toward the rostrum to say something the state chairman (who he understands in a sudden rush of feeling has been laying his wife for three months; it is one of the prices he has had to pay for his political career) pushes him to one side and makes the speech himself, only pausing now and then to look at the astronaut with amusement and approval as he tells the party assembled exactly what the astronaut's program will be.

"A new state, a new unity, a policy of conglomeration," the state chairman says, "a fusion of party and politics and personality in a union of destiny as slick and functional as a spacecraft, not the poison of the disparate personalities but the union of heart and will toward larger purposes," and so on and so forth and now—

the astronaut finds himself in a virtual montage of event: he dreams that he is criss-crossing the state in an attempt to cover all of its thirty-seven counties before his opponent can even get his program off the ground and in each and every one of them he identifies the opponent as the creation of the old machinery, an anachronism of a doomed age. At some of the stops he makes the speeches and at others he does not but every single night he lies with his wife in a motel room and falls into her breasts moaning. She does what she can but slips out around midnight in order to fuck the state chairman. (She is very level about this; she has long since told him that if he wants any marriage at all this is the basis it will now take and he has taken it, he carried her necklace to the Moon.) He meets an old man in a square who does not understand where the Moon was and the astronaut explains it to him genially as the media photograph it in two hundred degrees of lights for a sidebar. He meets Miss Licorice of 1973 in a swimming pool and she envelops him in gauze, crooning at him as he eyes her enormous breasts and says that there are peaks bigger than any on the Moon. (The media enjoy this.) The state chairman consults with him every morning but takes none of his advice and seems rather weary and distracted.

He dreams that on election night he sits in a hotel room above his headquarters and watches the results come in over television. He wins the election with fifty-five percent of the vote but as he turns to his wife for her approval he discovers that sometime during the evening she has left him and that the only people in his room are two large men with cold eyes who look at him with amusement when he says he must seek his wife. "Sit down friend; all the moves gonna be controlled now," one of them says giggling and the astronaut comes wearily to understand that he has, perhaps, lost control of the situation. Later, his wife returns and says that his son has fallen off a rooftop during a victory celebration but just as soon as the media are cleared out, aides will look for him.

The astronaut moves to touch her, but his hand seems to move through her body and lands against the cold flatness of the wall. It is the wall, then, which wakes him up, the wall which breaks him to understanding.

51

It feels like a bulkhead and the bulkhead was the ship and the damned ship staggering in space and so he wakes . up then at the beginning of his third week on Earth since he lost his mind and sent the command module back to home leaving his companions stranded crying on the Moon and the walls are dark here, the bed is warm and he lies there sweating for a long time, looking at the ceiling with eyes round and dull until the doctors come in accompanied at last by a General and he understands with release that finally they will arraign him.

V
THE FIRST COLONISTS 2036

A PREAMBLE

Mars does not exist. Nothing of this quality can. It is merely an abstraction within the Cosmic Mind which we seek so mendaciously—and hopelessly—to apprehend. That would be my roommate's theory. Since his training is in physics (a doctoral degree) and theology (his background is very painful), these thoughts should not be easily dismissed.

THE DESERT

It has long been established that the Martian atmosphere, being much thinner than that attracted by the bulkier gravitational pull of our own beloved Earth, cannot support life as we know it. That is, it will not support our lives as we remember them. Despite this accepted physical data, four men went out above ground the other day, removed their helmets, and died on the desert. It is clear that there was no foul play, for the search party found them lying in a neat tumble, their helmets placed at some distance from them on the sand. Apparently, this distance represents exactly that distance which a helmet-less man can travel from his equipment, say fifty yards. The names of these men were or are O'Toole, Goldberg, Szyncowski and Saltonstall, a splendid if rather funereal medley, reminiscent of certain archaic melodrama. The oldest was 25, the youngest 24. (We are rather a homogeneous community.) They were involved in the conversion of hydroponics to computer control but, apparently, had too much time on their hands, or what I may be trying to say perhaps is too little time on their hands.

STRAIGHT THROUGH THE COSMOS, BY THE DIVINING HAND OF TECHNOLOGY, TO OUR HUMBLE PROJECT

This morning, we received an official greeting from the President of the United States. Our radio is tuned to headquarters all the time, of course, but most of it is technical jargon, monitoring, patriotic reminiscences, popular tunes and so on for the specialists. At least twice a week, however, usually before our scheduled telecasts, a politician is given fifteen minutes or so to make a statement, and it is broadcast through the colony through the use of very special loudspeakers which are attached by clamps to most of the bedposts, tables and so on. Most of the statements are about the glory of it all and our responsibilities as free men and the sacrifices we are making on behalf of civilization and etc., materials which we try not to hear, but the President himself was both reasonable and sane: this was the first time he had spoken to us since the day of our swift debarkation some months ago, when he said that there was the beginning for all Mankind. This time he was even more eloquent; he said that the nation's hopes and prayers constantly followed our mission toward its successful completion and that all of us carried out the seed of hunger to that barren and strange place called Mars. "Do not forget that the great writer Ray Bradbury once reminded us that inside every man is a little clock ticking, ticking him toward his destiny, saying get out, get out. We do not yet know our destiny, of course, but we will find it if we only have the courage to voyage," the President reminded us. "Just as our pioneers voyaged so many centuries ago to find a better land and cleave a better life from the wilderness. From wilderness, that is to say." Because it was the President, the full colony, except for the necessary watch crews and maintenance personnel, was in its place listening. After the broadcast, some of us began faint but raucous cheering. It was not for what he had said, however, so much as for the fact that he had authorized us to give O'Toole, Goldberg, Szyncowski and Saltonstall a heroes' entombment at the base of the project, right next to the Martian artifacts. We had all secretly feared that he might, for some reason, identify them and call them traitors, but he took the whole thing very nicely, only alluding to the price of freedom and the inevitable sacrifices which had to be made. It was impossible to cover up the four deaths from anyone since Saltonstall and Szyncowski were fixtures of the broadcasts in their recurring roles of accordionist and free-verse spontaneous poet, both of them featured acts. I am not sure—having nothing at all to do with the communications and information division—but I suspect that they might have been informed that the four were killed by force or forces unknown. We could have gotten away with this because, despite most scientific evidence to the contrary, our politicans are mystics and do not totally reject, I am sure, the possibility of malevolent denizens of this planet coming from their shelters one night to balance off the tables. In that unfortunate happenstance, public opinion would have to be protected.

MY ROOMMATE AND I COME TO TERMS WITH ONE ANOTHER

My roommate is named Golding. Aaron S. Golding. He and I work in the so-called games-theory project, attempting to work out a systematized rule of chance which will map this planet by random means at the same time that it most equitably accomplishes division of labor for future and larger colonies. We can look forward, then, to generations of earthlike Martians, living by the patterns we will establish, but the truth is that so far absolutely nothing is really working out; all of the elaborate charts which had been researched on Earth seem utterly inapplicable to the situation faced here. Also, we are the only members of the project who do not need to be in this environment to accomplish our tasks, but some bureaucratic snare has never quite prepared for this, and so here we are, writing our own version of the great adventure. (Golding once admitted that he too kept a diary, an old habit he had picked up from ecclesiastical influence where students were required, in sanctuary, to take themselves apart now and then.) Golding says that this is all part of the celestial order of things: we are living evidences of the fact that all appearances to the contrary, we cannot yet quite revise our environment. "Indeed, there are things with which we dare not meddle," he says, which is strange because I remember his enthusiasm when he was selected for the colony and during all the preparations and ceremonies on Earth, he was in a state of the most positive ebullience, keeping up the spirits of those few of us who were having doubts. Perhaps the fact that he has had to leave a pregnant wife has something to do with this depression, but Golding insists that this is no fact of the case; it was a bad marriage in the first place and in the second he "only knocked the stupid bitch up so that we might have something left to talk about excuse the dangling prepositions. It is frightening, the strange ends to which we can turn the simple act of generation, but on the other hand, I didn't invent it, so it's not my responsibility." It is not, he adds, that he is anxious to return to Earth so much that he is afraid of the consequences of the project itself. I really do not know what to tell him; our specialty is mathematics, not philosophy or the physical sciences, and I left nothing myself on Earth other than that one illusion of consequentiality which sent all of us out here in the first place. Now, I have neither pretension nor hope; the death of the four men is inexplicable unless it is understood as being some extension of my own mood and yet, I cannot bear even now to think of myself as a murderer. Despite all this gloom, however, I am not at all suicidal: there is no question but that when we return to earth in six months I—and everyone else here—will be able to collaborate on a set of memoirs for large advance and might even become something of a celebrity. There are, after all, only sixty of us now left, one-sixteenth of the project having already phased itself on and the members of the first project did extremely well for themselves. There were fewer, of course. I have always been interested in writing a novel—mathematics was the safe choice for my parents, not the right one for me; what strange, timeless resentments!—and this might be one way into it. I have looked upon spaces and have seen sights never before, etc. Golding says that this protective stoicism is only a cover for the modal sense of terror which afflicts us all and he reminds me that the security precautions taken since the deaths would be utterly ineffective for anyone seriously determined, mathematically precise, religiously inclined.

AND, THUS TO LEAD A NORMAL LIFE

As far as possible, then, we carry on the twenty-four hour cycle of Earth and "night" falls every sixteen hours for all of the colony except rotating maintenance and watch crews. Lying in this huge dormitory, hearing the sounds all around me, it is impossible to believe that I am truly on Mars: I could be in boarding school or a particularly hideous version of army basic training: all of the shouts and cries of the sleeping men have to do with familiar terrors. "Mama mama!" and so on. They should have allowed the women on this second expedition but, of course, had their reasons. Our fear is the fear we have always known, our aspirations no different. Mars has nothing to do with it at all; we might as well be striking at gnats as Martians in our sleep-flail. It is for this reason that I feel my life here is essentially no different from anything that it ever was. I am unchanged.

ECOLOGY ON THE RED PLANET

Mars is not red but a concrete yellow, the dim, washed-out aspect of the coarse sands coming back, even through the filtered windows, as pain rather than apprehension. There are idle winds tracing here and there on all the spaces which kick the sand around and the desert is as far as we can see. I have never been "outside," have no urge whatsoever to go there, the only people who do are the exploratory teams who are especially trained for the treacherous surface. The unfortunate quartet were members of this crew. There are, to be sure, no rules against our leaving the dome—even after the accident we have only been encouraged to "use our judgment"—but the great majority here have never even thought of doing so; the irretrievable hostility of this planet is one explanation and the other is that there is plenty of work to do otherwise. Aided by our impressions and experiences, our relief colony may be more adventurous . . . although we understand from the broadcasts that they may be held up for somewhat more than the promised twelve weeks remaining of our shift. There seems to be some trouble down on Earth, we cannot quite get the details straight, but the Opposition leaders have focused, apparently upon the project as the cause of some social "unrest" and perhaps aided by this, certain elements of the population have caused "accidents" to befall unintentionally a couple of members of the replacement. We have rumors of bombings, threats, sabotage, nervous collapse and so on. All in all there is a point of view in the colony now that we may be held here for quite some time; we were warned of this risk of course and that of diminishing finite supplies, but it does seem ironic, as Golding now says, that it is not technological mishap which is problematic but only the same dreary

58

social malfunction which our triumphant quartet dealt with so admirably, if in such a mysterious way.

ANOTHER POINT OF VIEW

It is possible that rather than being bent on suicide, O'Toole, Goldberg, Szyncowski and Saltonstall might only have been trying to show us the way, were only trying to prove that, counter to the accepted data, man *could* survive unprotected on Mars. If that is true, then the removal of their helmets was a courageous, inspired act, one of those sheer, mad thrusts toward the unknown which have underlain all human breakthrough, and the throes of their deaths must have taken place in astonishment rather than depression. They had, perhaps, expected to walk back to the Dome and announce that we had misapprehended all physical and biological speculation. (So, give Mars a chance.) This means of course that one or several of them were crazy, but somehow the act becomes more accessible when seen this way. I can understand craziness. Golding puts it this way: "If we cannot carry out some piece of our constancy to the universe, if we cannot firstly be men, then perhaps we can never occupy the stars: these people were trying to prove their essential humanity, without which we are something less than men and it would not be human beings who can go out there. If you built a robot and he takes over Antares, has *man* occupied that star? Or is man merely the robot? I think that they were trying to show us that without the one there cannot be the other. Of course, this does not excuse the bad taste inherent in their heterogeneity of names, but I am convinced that this too was deliberate, that they meant to tell us something, and that even the most banal melodrama has some means of access to the cold, driven human heart."

THE WAY TO COME TO TERMS

Buggery to one side, Golding recommends masturbation; says that it is practically the best outlet available, and states that he has been practicing it quietly for several weeks without any fear of discovery; he suspects that more and more of us, afraid of the transistors and spies, are resorting to it rather than more florid contacts. This night, for the first time out here, I did it: I cleaned myself in the shower room that is, then, huddled in the spaces of my bed, searched for my prick and felt it curving into my hand, pawed it then and felt the old, slick, mean rising, found that with a few fumbles and tears I could wring myself to completion, speechless, within a matter of seconds.

At the moment of climax came not the image of a woman—which is an old problem—but only the blank spaces of this desert themselves; a yellow plunder beneath which are strewn, doubtless, the bones of thousands of creatures who came to extend their limits and found, instead, that it had worked in the other direction.

It is a strange thought, this, a strange sensation, and as I revolve onto my stomach, the feeling of coupling is enormous: it is as if my turgid, stuffed, faithful old prick were moving below me in a consciousness of its own, finding the perfect level of connection while the rest of me, stirring unknowingly above, has to settle for a more equivocal understanding.

VI
THE
CONQUEST OF
CONQUISTADORES
2423

ONE:

Entering the dock, Redleaf has a vision: the aliens will look exactly like his wife and their mouths bent into an accusatory *o* they will say to him, "What the hell are you doing in here looking like that? You barely have any right to the universe, let alone our quarters, you clean yourself up right this moment or we'll throw you out and take away your oxygen mask!" Or perhaps he is merely confusing one image with the other and is thinking of his mother again. The point is that neither he nor anyone else has ever been in a situation quite like this before, and he thinks that he is doing quite well, quite well, all things considered, in being able to come to significant terms.

TWO:

"Hello," the alien says as Redleaf shakes himself through the trap of the porthole. It has red eyes and a rather squarish countenance, otherwise it looks entirely—as the scientists would put it—humanoid. Perhaps there is a question of some intricate maladjustment of the limbs, and perhaps the alien's voice tends to squeak a bit, but it really is quite all right, it is almost comforting; it is very much within the ken of acceptable behavior. Redleaf feels enormously relieved, although the problem of negotiation remains ahead of him and he does not know if anything can be solved.

"You took a hell of a long time to get over here anyway, pal," the alien says, and when Redleaf starts, says, "Oh, didn't you know that? Your whole idiom and like that has been transcribed into us, we picked it up on our thought sensors which have been intercepting your communications for ages, we only thought that we'd better speak formally when we first made contact because it would keep your government cool. Actually, Johnny, we know everything: know every bit of the old argot. Why don't you drift in and make yourself comfortable, we'll rap for a bit and then after we've learned to hang loose we'll see what we can do." Dreamily Redleaf follows himself into the cubicle, reflecting that his agency, above all, would have little tolerance for the alien slang.

THREE:

Looking around the curiously homey surfaces of the room into which the alien has conducted him, Redleaf is reminded of nothing so much as his own living room at home; there is a couch, in the corner a table and some chairs, even a few execrable water-colors scattered around the walls, the poor taste and clumsy integration of the whole strikingly similar to that of his wife. Nothing quite works, it seems. Except for the unusual circumstances and for his strange companion, he could be sitting in his own home, feeling the slow slide of the day pulsing away from him, the dormant throb of the television set keeping the children quiet in the other room with news from Ganymede, the harsh whistle of his wife's breath as, with some skill, she worked over a code-puzzle. So much, so much to come from that to this; it is an irony which in other circumstances he is sure he could appreciate, if he were able, that is, to maintain that taste for irony which his wife says is something he has always lacked and which has made their life together so progressively intolerable.

FOUR:

"You see, Jack," the alien is saying, sitting at some cross-legged ease on the couch, facing him; Redleaf has taken one of the chairs, complaining that his bulky space suit makes him uncomfortable almost anywhere, "the thing is that we've been following you all these years, maybe 500 of your cycles, since you turned out post-technological anyway, and we've finally decided that you've reached a point where you're going to blow up the whole waxworks unless we can negotiate with you and bring you to our senses and get you to join our great conflagration. I mean confederation. Galactic confederation, that's the phrase I was looking for, we're still a little slow here on the uptake. The galactic confederation that is; all thinking and feeling races in the known universe belong to it except for a couple on the very outskirts like yourselves, and it's pretty clear, free and easy, wild stuff and mutual exploration, except for a couple of ground rules, nothing serious, otherwise that's the whole deal. Now what we want to do is to brief you up, take a load off your minds, get you to join our federation. You got to turn in the heavy weaponry and live good. You can keep the rockets, of course, that's fine. And you can have the whole solar system for a trade zone. There's nothing really worthwhile in it, it's kind of a depressed area if you dig what I'm saying. You wouldn't see us for eons and eons. But the weaponries. Those buggers gotta go. We can't take no chances. Of course we'll defuse them painless."

"But you don't understand," Redleaf says, rubbing his palms together in their steel, feeling the loss of callused contact as profoundly as he might notification of his own irreversible illness, "I'm not authorized to make any deal like that. I mean, I can't negotiate with you at all. I was merely sent as the emissary in answer to your request. My number came up in the program. I have no authority, all that I can do is convey—"

"Convey, shmonvey," the alien says, "what the hell's the big clatter? We make the pact with you and that's the end of the job, our boys move in and do their duty. All you got to say is the big word, give us that big yes, under law you see we gotta have the consent of one adult member of the planet, that's all. Just leave it to me, I'll swing the thing all the way. Yes or no? You can have the solar system and listen to this little concession I'm going to make you, now hear me out on this one: you can even have the radioactives too. All of them for peaceful purposes. We got to make a couple of adjustments on the half-lives and that's about it."

"You aren't clear," Redleaf says, "how you can reduce radioactivity in the one hand and let us keep the rocketry on the other. It doesn't sound too consistent to me."

"So what's a little fraud?" the alien says and shrugs. "You give me the big okay, we'll do it, and no one will ever know the difference. You don't need space anyway: every time you get so far out in it you fuck the whole thing up with a revolution or some such and get involved in social issues. So what the hell? It hasn't done a damned thing for you, we keep tabs you see, and in any event you're going about it the wrong way. Your technological thinking is, like, a thousand years in the past; there's a simple, cheap way you could get out to your planets without ever getting involved in all the hardware. It's just another way of looking at the problem and we'll be happy to help you. But anyway, the conflicts you got on that shithole will take you five hundred years to solve if you started on the proposition today, and who do you know that's going to be alive in even a hundred years? Immortality, incidentally, is impossible: you're practically at the maximum optimum span already down there. Not that

64

any of you really want to live longer anyway, it's all that you can do to put up with the chronology that you got."

"Listen," Redleaf says, "I don't like your attitude. Who are you to call my planet a shithole? Anyway, this was just supposed to be an initial exploratory contact and—"

"Well, it *is* a shithole," the alien says comfortably. "Nothing personal, you just don't know how to integrate your technology and the social network. We can teach you all that, it's very simple, and you don't have to kill more than a third of the planet painlessly at this point to work it out."

"I don't know about killing."

"Oh come on," the alien says. "You think that we can't work the thing out in a nice gentlemanly way? Modal point of relationships and all decisions is one to one to one to one you know, something which your technology must conceal in order to use up the excess bodies. You make the deal, that's it. Of course you know," the alien says and leans toward him, seems to wink, glitter against the twinkle of walls, "of course, Redleaf, there'll be a little something in this for you too. You understand that we don't do nothing without giving fair return. You want to get laid for instance?"

FIVE:

Once, hovering over his wife in the small doom of orgasm, Redleaf had thought that he had a vision, some signal profundity which would foreshadow the rest of his life: he was sitting at some vast remove in a position of security, administering irrevocable rules ... and this vision had come to him with such truth and clarity that the force of it alone had made him grunt; his wife had thought that he was still spilling and had considerably contracted but concentrate as he could upon it the vision would not stay (she was draining it away from him, the bitch), it drained away with his semen and he fell heavily upon her, panting slightly, seeing the shapes of the room spin around him and he realized then, against the thudding of his heart, that it had all been for nothing, nothing at all, merely a wisp of that fragmentary megalomania which sometimes came over him in the act of generation and which had no connection to history or outcome; it was merely glands, merely adjustments. He had no unusual destiny, his fate had been settled in his cells. Everything would always be the same and some day they would shoot him too for Titan from which he would broadcast back reports of sudden difficulty. Nothing would come of any of this. "Nothing, nothing," he had said to her and clasping her left breast, had begun to work himself into the rocking motions again, trying to force out of himself (as occasionally happened) the surprising twitch of another orgasm but none of that, none, none of that tonight, and so he had only slipped weakly out of her, moved against her belly, thinking of Titan, damned taunting moon, spinning in the frozen night, and he and the others on the ship, trapped in ozone, counting down for the transmitter as they sunk into the pit.

SIX:

"I don't mean to be a devil figure or a tempter," the alien is saying, "but after all, what did you expect up here? Gin rummy? We do business, that's our function and training. I've been manning this damned substation for forty years, give or take a little. It gets to be a bore. Can't beat around the bush. Got to flay the rabbit."

"Flay the rabbit?"

"Hit the course. Smash the apple. Who knows? Can't keep everything in your head, the goddamned idiom is so shapeless and *perverse*. It's always changing too. You can't stay even."

"You mean you're alone in this station?"

"Of course I'm alone. It's all civil service you know, all of it figured out in terms of retirement credits and so on and actually, if you have to know the truth, I'm a very junior member. Very junior. I'll get better posts and get back to the center of the galaxy and wind up being very well off, probably having something influential. But little mackerels make for big stews."

"Forty years?"

"Make it forty-two. No inconsistency, that's the way we live. We're patient and we really have very little to do with our lives anyway, so we might as well spend them observing. What do you say, Johnny? We give you the radioactives and you do what you want. Or we keep the radioactives and you get an action bonus. We can make you a hero or something like that or if you want we could even give you an inspection tour of the sector if you'd be interested in something like that. Our powers, in terms of your own limitations, are very, very strong. You want some money? We keep a bit of it up here for emergencies, more than you'd ever logically need."

"But so fast," Redleaf says. "You're making the whole thing happen to me so unbelievably—"

"Sooner we get this wrapped up, the sooner I can close the substation and get home," the alien says. He seems to be drooling slightly. "What do you say, we can work things out any way you want it and split the difference down the line. All the same to me. Give us the word and I'll move the big babies in to exert a little payload."

"I don't know," Redleaf says. This happens to be almost the truth. "I just don't know."

SEVEN:

In the briefing they had reminded him that he was going up as the best hope of mankind and that once he consented to greet the alien there was no turning back. He was committed to the mission. They had reminded him of television, however, and of the lucrative book and magazine contracts that would come to him as a result of the chance. "There are others, of course," they had told him, "lots of others who would do this; we're just picking you because you seem a shade the most qualified, but if you don't want to go you don't have to," and he had said "no, no, I'll go," and had told them that he would serve the best purposes of earth in making a contact with the aliens who had been signalling them, and his first thought, actually the very first thought when he left the briefing, was that if he got through it he would probably be able to parlay his way out of the mess, somehow vault himself entirely clear of it and toward some clear element of possibility where the project would not matter, Mars or Titan would not matter, the whole agency or his wife would not matter, it would only be him alone and with the breeze of increase always on his face, although about twenty years too late for that, twenty years too late kid and don't you ever, ever forget that.

EIGHT:

"I can't do it," Redleaf says and fumbles for the weapon in his suit. Hot and heavy and clumsy work but he finds it. "I simply can't do it; I got far too much integrity, I got to think of Earth and our future precious generations of adorable unborn children," and drills the unprotected alien through what could be the heart.

The alien's eyes widen, he twitches, he collapses moaning before Redleaf, spilling blood, spilling little bits of tissue, his very brain seeming to expectorate in agony through his lips as he tries unsuccessfully to gasp out something, then rolls on its front, twitches and is still. Redleaf pockets the weapon with a sense of satisfaction, perhaps it will be said in future generations that he is the man who has saved the Earth and he guesses that he can come to terms with that either way; certainly he will not be an anonymity anymore. He is distinguished from the others on the project. He turns on his radio and, speaking into the small wrist microphone says, "I got him. I got him good."

"That's splendid," says a thin high voice. "Glad to hear it. That means you passed the test."

Then for a long, long time they speak to him soothingly about Titan, about qualifications, about the imagination and courage he has shown under hypnotically-induced stress but Redleaf, turned off of it, hears nothing, says nothing, looks glumly into the darkness as the lie they have told him begins to crumble and he understands, after a fashion, that nothing will save him from the pit of Titan other than the alien which they have constructed and which he has blown out of the universe.

VII

AN INTERVAL IN THE ADVENTURE, 1999

There's nothing really doing on the Moon.

There hasn't been for some time, you know. The resort business was good for a while and there was a certain novelty appeal to the whole gig—expanding the frontiers of the universe and finding our destiny and so on—but it faded away rapidly. Nowadays, Washington Compound is practically vacant except for the hundred or so (it's a damned stable population) who hang on for their subsidized make-it and the outlaw colonies who are rumored to be adapting to life in the craters. Me, I can't stand the place.

I haven't even been off the ship to see it for the last six months, due to certain regrettable events. I don't miss it. Considering the fact that we make the jaunt twice a week, back and forth, with a two-hour layover, I suppose that this is an unusual admission.

The Moon might have been something in the old days

when I was ten or fifteen or so, I'll say that. It has the look. Some of the cabins and villas under the Dome have a rococo elegance and, even through the masks, I swear that I could smell the residue of old litter through the surrounding spaces. It has the aspect—the whole thing now—of Coney Island late on a July Sunday after a particularly crowded weekend, and although I'm hardly an expert on the Moon—just the motorman on the shuttle, that's me—I sure as hell know about Coney Island. I go there every so often and there's more action there on a bad Friday than there ever has been in the whole history of the Moon, and I'm not averse to action. Of most kinds.

The trouble with the Moon, the way I see it, is that it was a fad and like most of those crazes, it ran out quickly, past a point of diminishing return. Now they're all thinking about Mars, but a lot of people who I know personally got sunk in real estate and various kinds of speculation which surrounded the nonsense of 1980 and got hurt very bad. The Moon as the new frontier, the Moon as the next barrier for tourists to crack and so on. The same old manipulative shit. The whole campaign was, of course, cooked up by no more than twelve clever people in a total of maybe four offices and after they cleaned out, there was very little left. Certainly, little enough left on the Moon. The entire experience of commutation is absolutely depressing, and although I tell my wife I'm lucky to have it—I'm close to forty and distinctly too old for Mars, which is a much, much better buck—the fact is that I do look forward very much to the opportunity to retire at the end of the year. I won't quit before that because it would blow the pension but I'm not asking for any extension. The retirement pay will be pretty fair and what I actually want to do is to retire to the country and get involved in livestock. That's where the future is, in food. I can see it coming.

Cows as companions would compare favorably to the bohemian colonies which are the last outpost of human energy on the Moon. As I say, there are about a hundred of these "people"—loosely organized into about ten of what they call "clans"—living under the dome in all kinds of peculiar relationships and with little reference to those realities which put them there in the first place. A lot of courage and sacrifice, for instance. Generally speaking, these are the children of the resort people who went broke; they hang on because they had been raised there, and staying is easier for most of them than going back to Earth and making something of themselves in the New Economy. Despite the huge costs of maintenance under the Dome, however, the Government is largely willing to foot the expense because, for whatever reason, the bohemians keep us short of total evacuation (I am not counting those who live in the craters themselves; that is virtually a different species and any contact with them at all would be highly risky) and it is not in human nature to admit to a disaster as total as I think the Moon boondoggle was.

Congress some years ago, then, voted cheerfully for the massive appropriations that keep my little crew, my ship and myself trundling in the darkness to drop off supplies and good news at their end and to bring home an occasional corpse and bad news from there. Bohemians are all the time getting cut up in their so-called "feuds" and the Government has been very strict upon the matter of Moon burials. There will be none. Perhaps, and here I am giving only one man's opinion, perhaps the true horror of the swindle only assaults us at the moment of someone's death there; to bury on the Moon would be a complete severance from our history.

This is little more than a thought. I'm not very good at this sort of thing and my job places no premium on making up my own mind about almost anything at all.

THE REASON I HAVE NOT BEEN OUT ON THE MOON FOR SIX MONTHS

The reason that I have not been out on the Moon for six months has to do with certain events which occurred the last time that I went out. As a matter of fact, it was an experience which made me swear off the Moon forever. I am perfectly willing to sweat out a pension running a freight-and-hearse service ... but there is no reason at all to get involved with the subjects on one end, and I came to that decision without any regrets the time I saw the bohemian couple lying locked with one another on the very edges of the Dome. I found myself walking directly toward them on my last time through and I was damned if I was going to turn to their convenience. Why should I? Do they own the Moon because they occupy it?

They were literally perched up against the wall, the disgusting creatures, as close to fucking I suppose as it is possible in heavy Moon gear, and quite oblivious to my approach. The boy had removed some of his bottom castings and arranged his helmet in some sort of a strange way so that it concealed all of him but his mouth. One of their newer perversions. The girl was lying straddled across him, her face in his lap, her hands somewhere in the vicinity of his shoulder-joints. I could see his thighs bucking and thrashing at her, the lout. Well, they have no shame.

Not that it made any difference to me at all. They can do what the hell they want down there, as far as I'm concerned it is behavior fit for the Moon. But I caught a piece of rock in a heel and went down, slowly, on my posterior, and there was something of a clatter.

When I scrambled to my feet, and somewhat embarrassed about it all, they had broken apart and were staring at me.

"What are you doing here?" the girl said through her transmitter. "Who are you?"

"I'm the commander of the *Endeavor*," I radioed back, "and I'm taking a walk around the Dome. What's the difference? Am I bothering you? You two seem to have been making out quite nicely."

"What's the difference this one asks," the girl said. She turned to the boy. "Tell him what the difference is."

"I know you," the kid said. "You're the bastard that comes by every week and makes speeches to us about how we're all escapists and we should come back to face your kind of reality. I know you damned well. You're my brother, my soul, my companion."

"I don't care what you do," I said. "I really don't." I

73

meant it, at least in the particular. Although I can make efforts, now and then, to talk sense to some of them in groups, it is really none of my business what these perverts want to do. For that matter, it is hardly my fault that service compels me, now and then under the contract, to give a kind of re-enlistment talk to these troops. "You can stay here and grow old for all I care. Become all of 25. You can even bring children onto the Moon if they can stand it. You seem to be giving it a try, anyway."

"Get this," the girl said in a high voice. "Listen to the bastard. He thinks he's clever."

"I don't like idiots," the boy said, coming slowly to his feet and tilting his helmet so that I could see the eyes. "I don't like them on my territory and I particularly don't like asinine platitudes. I'm just coked up enough to beat the shit out of this guy if you don't mind, Deborah."

Deborah. They all have names like *Deborah* or *Polonius* or *Armstrong.* That was the phrase when the first families came out with children.

"I don't mind at all," she said. "As a matter of fact, I'd like to sit and watch this through."

"Now, listen," I said, "I don't even know who the two of you are. Outside the Dome I have nothing to do with you at all. I was just taking a walk and I'm going back to my ship. So let's adjourn this. Do." As you see, I was trying to be reasonable. I am a reasonable man. Even with scum, I know that taking the moderate line pays.

"Sure he's going back," the girl said. "Into the little ship and up into the big sky. What do you want to be when you grow up, the first man to land on Mars?"

But you can't be decent. They'll get you every time, although you should know better. I felt the old, painful, congested rage moving within me and I think that all things being equal at that time, I might have hit her, but the boy got to me first.

He caught me with a sneak punch behind the right ear where the metal is too thin for that kind of thing, and he must have knocked me out for a moment because the next thing I knew, I was already in the process of getting up and he was looking at me, leering. I was in pain. His

74

eyes, full and round, seemed to take that terrible knowledge from me, but what he did was to hit one fist against the other first instead of coming right in. They are arrogant and easily trapped by their own stupidity. I could hear the metal clang.

"Good," he said. "That's a good start. Get ready, friend, because here it comes again."

"No," I said. "Please don't do it. I'm warning you now, I don't want to get involved with you scum but you'd better not try a thing more. If you do——"

"Get that," he said, and threw a fist at me, missed, and poised again. "Dig this shit."

That was when I lost control. "You trash," I screamed, and took my gun from the inner pocket and shot him, just once, in the head. The projectile went all the way through, of course, just as the manual said it would. These armaments are marvelous.

He fell in front of me.

"He's dead," the girl said. "You killed him." She had no expression in the voice, it was as if she was trying to find the right attitude to come into me with.

But I was still concentrating on the bastard. "You son of a bitch," I said and shot him again, for good measure, then in the fit that I could barely understand but had had too often to resist, I turned on the girl and raised the gun to her eyes.

"You want it too?" I said.

She shook her head and said nothing. I could see her eyes rolling and she staggered back.

"I could do it, you know. I don't have to put up with this kind of thing from scum. Nobody wants you. Back on earth, you don't even exist except as a kind of convenient statistic. I could wipe out the whole damned colony and say that it was one of your feuds and that would be the end of the whole thing. There wouldn't be any replacements. Everybody who would be on the Moon is *on* the Moon now."

"No," she said, still backing. "No, no. What's wrong with you? Don't you understand what's going on here?"

I understood everything but was too far gone. They

had touched, together, that reservoir of pain, grief, need within me. And they'll do it to you every time, too, long past any point when you can take it any more. They know the pressure points. It's the only thing left in them.

"I won't put up with it, you see," I said to her flatly and shot the girl through the heart. She fell before me soundlessly, the metal of her suit gliding to rock as if it were rubber.

I was still angry. I could have incinerated the Moon itself if I had had the equipment. Instead, I settled for incinerating the two of them with the beam on high. There was nothing to it at all. Just a little bit of betraying ash which I spread with my boots around the Dome.

Then I managed to put the gun away and got back to the ship.

I thought about filing a report on it, but decided not to: they could as likely have killed each other. Probably, they would have, eventually, if I hadn't interceded. No, I simply put a note in the log to that effect—that I had found some suspicious ash around the Dome which might be human in origin but felt no need to investigate further—and left it at that. There wasn't anything to it at all. There never is.

I haven't been outside since. My two-man crew brings the mail and messages back to me. I know perfectly well that the colony knows what happened and what I did, but that's all right with me because there's nothing that they can do. The filth; their word means nothing to Earth and I transmit all their word anyway. And if one or ten of them ever wanted to go back to report what happened, they'd have to go with me.

I'd take care of them.

The hell with the whole boondoggle. My year ends in three months and then I am going.

Aside from the events I've transcribed here to explain my feelings, nothing ever happens on the Moon.

IN THE HOT PLANET, 2117

Coles and I are down on Mercury. It was a difficult landing and a perilous climate and now that we are down, there is really very little to do, but who am I to question any of this? The point is that we have accomplished man's second landing on the hot planet, aided by technology and great personal courage and now they want to talk to us.

"Put the damned transmitter on," Coles said. The green light is flashing, indicating that they want to get through. "You want them to put the video on and see what is really going on here?"

In truth, I do not. Coles, unshaven, is lying naked on his bunk, working out a cryptogram, and I am in no particular state of dress myself. The temperature in the cabin is only seventy degrees, but there is something about the psychic effect of outside temperature which keeps us very hot all the time. Coles, a heavy man, is in a sweat. I am not that far gone but feel a burning and itching in the skin.

"Put the damned thing on," Coles says again, more loudly. The fact is that I do not like him very much. Although we were selected for compatibility and although our position on this voyage is mutual, there is a question of personal antagonism which goes far beyond the technology. Coles is crude, simple-minded, goes in for pornographic illustrations and long raving monologues about his drinking adventures, carried on right under the very noses of the directors of the Program. For a time this amused me—Coles, after all, appears to have gotten away with a great deal and the pictures themselves are very interesting —but there is a certain point in situations like this, past which the novelty of contact passes. We have been together for two weeks and have already broken down into incivility. Perhaps the basic problem was designating me as the senior and nominal commander of the expedition; equal rank would not have led to such tension. Of course, I am more capable and have more seniority than Coles. I do not deny this.

"Put the fucking thing on!" he says again and I do so, flicking the switch for reception. That they can pick *us* up all the time is not doubted, although they have never come out and said this, and all of the training was curiously mute about the degree to which Control could monitor conversations in the spacecraft. At first we were concerned about this, but it is surprising how quickly it wore off. Now we say anything to each other we please, some of it, I would suspect, quite seditionist in intent. It is a peculiar fact to acknowledge, but Coles and I, at this point, are practically revolutionaries. We see no point in the system as it has worked out in the practice: certainly the effects it has had upon us are against the spirit.

"Receiving, Willis?" Control says, and I say, "We're receiving." "How are you, Coles?" the voice asks, and Coles says "I'm all right," and then nothing more. The onus, it would seem, is upon Control.

There is a slight pause, faintly awkward, and they say, "Are you settled in down there? We haven't heard from you in a couple of hours."

"We have completed procedures," I say. "Thermosts are checked. Escape rockets have been prepared. Oxygen system is normal. Hydroponics tank reacting normally." The hydroponics is a new innovation. We are the first ship to carry them; they are testing hydroponics for the Centauri run. Of course the Centauri run is several centuries away but there is nothing like being prepared. Already they have completed the hydroponic and tranquillizing equipment.

"That's fine," Control says.

"Tell them to fuck themselves!" Coles roars from the couch.

This is a habit which Coles has fallen into recently. Control makes little of it because, since the Venus disaster, it has been agreed that self-expression is important in space, and the crew, within certain limits, must be allowed to express itself as it wishes. Of course obscenity is still outlawed for the broadcasts.

"Willis," Control says. "We have a request for you." For some reason the voice sounds shy, a little bit tentative. Are they going to ask us to sing songs again on the next broadcast? "We'd like you to do a broadcast now. A general transmission. A full hookup."

"That's ridiculous," I say. "We just gave them a broadcast, four hours ago, when we landed. We were on for four hours. Enough is enough."

"I know."

"We aren't scheduled for a full twelve hours," I say. "We've got to get our rest, you know."

"Tell them to shove it up their asses!" Coles shouts. He takes his deck of playing cards from beside him and flings it at the blank viewscreen. "We got the same rights in space as the rest of them, you can look it up."

"I'm sorry," Control says. It seems to be barely whispering. "We wouldn't ask you if these weren't emergency circumstances. We're having a little—uh—trouble in some of the cities. We feel it would be best if you could do a hookup and—uh—talk to them a bit."

"It's another goddamned revolution," Coles says. "Don't you think they'd have a week's worth of peace before it all started again? How many riots can they take up there? Don't they ever run out of energy?" He stirs on the bunk, thrashes a bit, and for a moment I think that he is on the point of getting up, but then he subsides, grunting. Coles is a good man for gestures, but the point is, his technological expertise to one side, he has very little follow-through.

"We did talk to them," I say. "We talked to them five times on the way here and we talked to them all the way down to the surface of the planet, and we've given them more tours of the ship than we have plants in the hydroponics assembly, and I just don't think that there's anything more to say. I'd like to help, but—"

The fact is that the riots have reached a state of such continuousness now that it is almost impossible to get excited about them, and the fact is that I am surprised at Control. Dysfunction has become a way of life, or, as Coles says, there are more people convinced that the Government is inimical to their lives and functioning than indifferent to it. In such circumstances, dislocation is inevitable. The point is that it hardly matters any more, and that nothing, truly, changes.

"Well," Control says, "well, Willis, you've got us in a very tough spot, you see. I mean, I might as well come out and tell you the truth. The thing is that they want to seize the transmitters and stop the broadcasting, they want to stop the communications belt."

"That's nothing new," I say.

"Well," Control says, "well, ah, Willis, how can I put this to you and to Coles so that you can truly understand, ah, let me say that they have, uh, *friends* located in a position to help them with this, ah, objective. They want to pull the plug, Willis. What's going to happen then? The thing is, we think that if you or Coles could talk a bit, maybe do a video and speak some sense to them, things might quiet down. You aren't without influence, you know."

"How about that?" Coles says. He does get up from the bunk now, wanders over to my side, smelling hideously, and looks at the speaker with serious interest. "They can't even keep things quiet for a few days down there? Can't you do anything competently, Control?"

I should point out that all voices who deal with us refer to themselves and are addressed merely as *Control,* and we are unaware of specific identities. The break between the exploration and broadcasting crews was legislated some years ago as the dangers of emotional involvement had been made quite clear in certain aspects of the Venus disaster. For that reason, Control's appeal lacked the emotional force or poignance which it might have had at other times, in different circumstances.

"Personally, I think you fuckers might as well burn," Coles says. "Our job is just to make a landing on this planet and certain observations, you know. We don't really have to make a show of it. Remember, that whole thing was settled years and years ago. We don't owe you anything except the performance of our duties."

"I'm speaking to Willis," Control says. "I think that he's the man to deal with in these circumstances. Unless you feel—"

"Ah, blow it out your rear end," Coles says and slaps the microphone absently, goes grunting to the rear of the cabin. The gesture is not as effective as it might be in other circumstances because the cabin is quite small and there is very little space to put between us, but nevertheless he tries. The fact is that, although Coles knows his job very well and is an excellent engineer, he has quite a poor taste for public relations, even poorer than my own. In the old days, there is no chance that he would have been allowed to participate. I believe that his basic problem is that in intellectual terms he is simply not very bright, but I have not quite worked this out to my entire satisfaction. It is one of the many things which will go into this series of notes which I am writing, to be released after the project comes to a successful conclusion.

"Willis?" Control says. "Willis? Are you there? Don't do this, Willis. Cut it out, Willis. You've got to be reasonable and cooperate. I'm telling you, if they get in here—"

"Oh, the hell with it," I say. I feel grudging, of course, but it is to be admitted that Control's desperation and the nakedness of their plea has filled me with a sense of power. It is humbling to realize, after all, how much we are carrying out in these explorations and to be a participant in the second landing on Mercury is no small thing, it will probably stand up in the long run. "I don't care. We'll do a broadcast. Just let us clean up for a few minutes or so and we'll go on for a short while. A short while."

"We'd appreciate that. Could you try to slant it in favor of reason? You know what we mean, Willis. Talk about the necessity for moderation and slow social change and so on and so forth and how your lives are dependent upon keeping the communications belt clear. Well, you know what I mean."

"I'll handle it the way I want to," I say. "You'd better count yourself fortunate that we're willing to cooperate this far. The fact that you can monitor us all the time doesn't mean that you can *do* anything," I remind him, and with a quick flick of the wrist, shut off the voice. I look out the window and perceive, through the shading, that Mercury, as usual, seems very hot and foreboding, although there are few physical details to be made out in the haze. It would be possible to believe that the entire constitution of this planet was liquid if we were not, uneasily, on solid ground somewhere. "What the hell?" I say to Coles. "It doesn't cost us anything and we can bail them out of a tough spot down there."

"I'm getting sick of these riots," he says, sitting down on his bunk, shaking his head, looking abstractedly for some clothing which, possibly, he has placed under his pillow. "Riots, riots, all the time upheaval. How the hell can they expect to send men out to Mercury if they can't even control a simple situation down on Earth? They ought to knock their heads in."

"It's not that simple," I say and would go on to remind Coles about the various and intricate social situation which in so many ways has made it impossible to determine whether there is a government and an anti-government or merely two governments, co-existing in rather malevolent distaste, with the one of them putting its emphasis on the technology (some of which it owns) while the other has rather more suspicions about the same technology (some of which it owns). It is an interesting topic, one of my particular fields of emphasis, but Coles is quite right in only making a gesture and saying, "Well, hell, if we have to do this, let's get it the hell over with," and I agree, going to the mirror which lay over one of the bunks so that I can check out certain details of my appearance; meanwhile Coles has found his clothes and, grunting, is getting into them. "Nonsense," he is muttering, "absolute nonsense," and my deepest tendency is to agree, but the fact that Coles and I have gotten along so poorly on this trip and really have purposes which are in such opposition makes it impossible for me to sympathize. "What the hell?" I say, "we can function as a good example." "That's the whole problem," Coles says, "making an example of us, why the hell should we be an example? It's only a question of doing a job, I don't see why we have to be something to live up to as well." I point out that the job itself is somehow questionable, but Coles, who for all his bulk and crudity is something of a speculative type, is well launched into the metaphysics of the thing and won't stop. "You see, the whole thing got off the wrong way," he says, "it became a means for the government, the governments, I should say, to beat up the populace, make examples of the men who were in the program as being right types and in the bargain make the government stand up, everything that was done wasn't done for space but only for the government and when you get started that way you don't get off the track easy." Again I point out to Coles that this is not quite the fact of the case; for one thing, men like the two of us would hardly be permitted as the second Mercury expedition if the government was merely interested in code-heroes, but Coles simply shakes his head and mentions that the Venus disaster things have somewhat loosened up, but not in any basic way. "The thing is that what you do is still an instrument of social control," he says, and then, putting his hair in place, he adds, "Well, let's get the damned thing over with." Strangely reluctant at this moment, I nevertheless agree and put on the transmitter, say, "We're ready now if you are," and after an interval, Control says, "We're all ready for you, Mercury. Networks have been cleared. Transmission belt is open. Put on your viewscreen."

We turn on the camera in the cabin with a switch. Automatically the lights dim, adding a hazy, not unromantic flush to the background, and I rub my cheeks absently, realizing that I have forgotten to put on the make-up. At this juncture, I suppose, it hardly matters, but some intimation of loss of precision unsettles me and I find myself momentarily unable to speak, sit before the camera in a slow stun of embarrassment until it is Coles who saves the situation, coming beside me, pointing rather forcefully and saying, "Well, good evening, Earth. Good evening once again from the planet Mercury." A belch settles in him, he covers his mouth, doubles up slightly and then comes erect. "It occurs to us that some of you aren't precisely behaving yourselves up there; some of you have got the wrong attitude on the project here. So let me explain.

"Let me explain," Coles says and gestures rather floridly; I realize then that he's drunk. How he was able to sequester pills and get them into his metabolism under the monitoring of Control is beyond me, but nevertheless his mood is high, detached, somewhat wanton; the thing is that he is addressing the camera exactly as he was me, "Let me try to explain a few things so that you come to your senses. In the first place this is a very hazardous mission, we don't talk about that but it's behind the scenes all the time, *very* hazardous, and the fact that men have already landed on Mercury safely does not mean that this is duck soup. We could die at any time, technological mishap, failure of the re-entry or escape rockets, anything like that at all. So that's one thing to look forward to. And in the second place, this is very serious stuff here: you've got to understand that, this isn't heroics, this here is a serious scientific mission during which we're trying to evaluate Mercury for exploration and so on and so forth. Maybe we can live on Mercury, who knows? We need space somewhere; it's getting more and more crowded up there. The fact is that we've got to look to the future, stop mucking around in the past, be progressive. We've got to think of all the angles, the implications, the promises and depth. The Moon wasn't colonized in a day you know and it wasn't our fault it worked out that way. Now what we're doing here, we're doing for all of you, don't you see that?"

"Of course," I add. "That is a point worth making, that this is a joint investigation of space, joint in the sense that it unites not only the explorers but the explorers and the race itself, we're doing it for all of you and—"

"Oh, shut up, Willis," Coles says, and backhands me, pushes me half-painfully away from the range of the camera. "That's my companion here, George Willis. Willis is supposed to be commander of this expedition but how can you have a commander with only two people? Why does there always have to be a superior and an inferior even in the most microcosmic situations, can't we simply deal with each other? Well, we won't speculate; that's another issue entirely, we can talk about it next Wednesday or slightly before. No, consider my friend Willis for a moment. Speculate on him long and hard, he is no simple creation here. Willis has at great personal risk taken himself to Mercury, left his wife and family and the bosom of his home to voyage out among the stars—well, to voyage out among the planets anyway—and he had done all this in the belief that it is real and earnest and that behind him there is a base of knowledge and dignity and composure and so on and so forth. He is not a simple man, Willis! He does nothing without gauging its effects! What he has done, he has done for you! Would you disappoint him? Would you do anything down there to indicate to this man that he is living a lie and that his purposes are as extraneous as they are deadly? Of course you wouldn't, in the words of Willis himself, you believe every word of this! Every single word! So our request to you from the hot and gaseous sands of Mercury tonight, or do I merely mean today, well, whatever the hell time it is, my request to you is that you ponder long and hard upon the implications of what you have heard tonight and that you understand that there is nothing simple about this. Later on, perhaps, my friend Willis will take you on a guided tour of the hot planet. We can turn the cameras outside, you know; there's no reason why you have to look at us all the time. We can show you the deadly trap of this planet, a planet so deadly—mark this, people!—a planet so deadly that a single breath, *one single breath,* one merest inhalation of its atmosphere, would render every human being dead, that is to say, if every human being were breathing this stuff, oh, a very deadly planet, menacing and ugly, Willis will show you all of it if you behave reasonably and, in fact, if your behavior is perfectly reasonable, if we get good reports from Control, Willis, my friend here, Willis might be induced to wander out in camera range and there, on the surface of the planet itself, to remove his helmet—*remove his helmet*—and take a breath for the sake of all humanity! Wouldn't that be wonderful? Isn't that something to be thankful for? Think of it, think of it well," Coles says and stops, looks at the camera with a curiously blank and fixated expression, shakes his head, gasps, and retreats to his bunk out of camera range where he sits with his head buried in his hands. He has, it would seem, turned the format over to me, and it occurs to me that I have absolutely nothing to say; that Coles has said it extremely well, at least from his point of view, and that anything I would add would be entirely, or at least partially, superfluous.

"Well," I say, "well, I think that's very well put and I do hope that there won't be any violence, no violence at all," and with that I flick off the camera, turn us out of view range and join Coles to sit hip to hip on the bunk. We are still in range, of course, they can hear our breathing and anything we might say. Accordingly I say nothing, nor does Coles, we merely sit there for a very long time in a mutuality so perfect and timeless that it goes beyond any necessity for communication, and when Coles begins to giggle, the sound is so unexpected that it comes with the impact of rifle fire; then Coles gets up, walks to the main lock, unseals the bolts and opens the exit hatch. He does this quickly and deftly and with an utter sense of purpose. I would not stop him even if I wanted to, the precision of his movements is so beautiful. Watching Coles clamber through the hatch and onto the saddle of Mercury I feel as I did many years ago when I saw my father on the beach moving at a great distance into the deadly surf, his arms poised, his head bent, his body crooked, as if to receive a caress, but caress or deadly blow alike, it all would have been the same as he slipped into the waves and vanished, perishing with such finality that it was conceivable that he would never again return to pick me off the beach. Which he did. Or did not. I have not quite figured this out yet.

FUCKDAY SIX, 2402

Lying cross-angled by the whore, feeling the slow, almost ominous unwinding of his genitals beneath him, Sanders has a notion: a notion unlike almost any of the others which he has had this day and which in its profundity and gloom stops him cold, causes him to gasp, jiggle, remove himself from her. It is as if, he has decided, the whole thing is dreamlike; yes, that is precisely the point, none of this is really happening at all, or, worse yet, it is happening in some small, enclosed space of his mind, far beyond the sense of things, which is large, peripheral, and entirely grey. Sunlight comes in like a rope through the windows, dappling her body momentarily, and he tries to crush himself against a nipple, tries to immerse himself beyond conception once again, but it is no good, his brain has once again run away with his mind—this is an old problem—and with a whinny of disgust he turns from her, pivots on an elbow, sits on the bed with something approaching a flounce and looks at her in the clean light, trying to understand exactly what is happening to him, not that knowing it would change anything, of course. Of course.

"What's wrong, baby?" the whore says, and then her own mood imperceptibly shifts; like most of them she has caught not speculation but rejection in his gesture (they are always, always the same, their difference is an illusion propounded by cosmetics) and she blinks her eyes at him, runs a finger over his chest and says, "Don't tell me you're one of them, too. Hope not. You can't find a man in ten who can keep it up those days. Even when they are paying for it. It's a strange thing."

"Nothing personal," Sanders says because of course it isn't: she is really a very nice whore as whores go, what with having offered herself on the street without any abashment or the kind of manipulation which most of them cannot abandon, even on a fuckday. But this one had merely said to him, *you look like you want a woman; let's go to my room,* and had left it at that with a nice honesty and not at any time since he put his arm around her, took her to this hotel, removed her clothes and his and straddled her has there been any question of money, not even raised by inference. She means, apparently, to meet the conditions of the day to the letter, which is a relative rarity. Nevertheless, even now, particularly under these circumstances, he feels himself capable of nothing other than slow conversation, perhaps a little communion, a shade of realization ... nothing else. "I'm just not in condition for it," he says, wondering if he can make this metaphysical point distinct to her from that simple impotence she would know so well and thinks she has located. "I got things on my mind. I mean to say, I caught myself thinking."

"No thinking," she says and puts a heavy arm around him, draws him against her, extends with a palm a long, drooping breast whose nipple he begins to suck without inference, without any sense of goal, but suddenly her hands are insistent, moving around his prick to cup and extend him and there really is nothing to do. He cannot, in the last analysis, get out of this except through the obvious route. He begins to work on her purposefuly, driving his body against her, forcing his hands around and through her crevices, trying then to force himself into some simulacrum of connection which will serve as well as the real and which, once accomplished, will leave him free once again to consider all the implications of precious fuckday and what it is doing to all of the peoples of the world. That was one of the conditions of it, like the Days of Mourning, you had to think about it and try to understand what it meant. Somewhere, buried at the dead-center of his contemplation, he knows, is an insight so enormous as to toss the whole thing into final perspective, but the whore is demanding and he is slow and the music of his juices is grinding and the odds are, the possibilities very much so, that there will come at the end of this, only an orgasm so draining, in fact so entirely devastating, that he will be unable to think of anything else, which is, of course, an ancient habit. There are a lot of ancient habits hanging around this bed at this moment: old cunning, old deception, old lies in the night and he hopes that he will learn to survive all of them as he drives finally inside her, feeling his loins contract like a puppet's limbs as he begins the squeezing, pumping motions which are at the core of any truly cherished understanding of fuckday.

On Ganymede: Feuer picks up the microphone, thumbs it over and says, "All right, we've just settled here now into a long, shallow crevice. I would estimate it as being about two miles across, maybe couple feet deep, the ship is rocking a little but no real problems. We're in! We're into Ganymede! We made the moon of Jupiter!"

Perhaps his enthusiasm has been too limited. Or perhaps problems of transmission across this many millions of miles block out any quality of emotion. In any event, Control says, "You sure about that Feuer? We still sense a little elevation in the radar back there. Watch that respiration-rate. Your heartbeat is coming over a little wild. Slow, even breaths."

"Positive," he says, trying to breathe slowly. "Absolutely positive. We verify a dead-settle."

"Well. All right then. How's Green; did he make the impact all right? Report if necessary."

Feuer looks at his sleeping partner curved on the seat next to him, the shallow whimpers of respiration coming out of him harshly and says, "He seems to be all right for the moment. It was quite a gentle landing." Green had gotten sick somewhere beyond Mars and by twelve hours within the Ganymede landing had been totally incommunicative, lapsed deep into what Feuer supposed to be a coma but there was, of course, no way of turning the craft, not that in any event Control would have heard of it . . . basically it is a one-man mission anyway, no evacuation of the craft, no real maneuvering, the two of them are put in there only for dialogue and to keep Control diverted and Green, therefore, will have to make out as best as he can. It is no one's problem. Feuer hopes that whatever the man has got, it is not communicable, but he rather doubts it: more than anything else he thinks that it is *angst* which got Green on his first trip beyond the orbit of Mars, not that this would move toward any workable understanding of the universe or, for that matter, of Green himself.

"He'll make it," he says to Control, knowing that Control could not be less interested in Green, or is he only thinking of himself: is everything himself? and Control some kind of projection of his own condition, wandering two hundred and fifty million miles behind?

"Well, hold on then," the transceiver says. "Just sit pat now and don't try any further procedures. We'll have the President on with you in just a second, and I think he'll want to say a few important words. Now remember, Feuer, play it down, anything he says is fine with you, and you like his image. There's no reason to pull any of that antagonistic crap and besides he's a very nice, sensible kind of guy if you can only get to know him. He's under a lot of pressure too, remember that."

"I never knew him."

"No one knows him, but that doesn't mean he can't be good to deal with. If he wants to talk to Green, tell him that he's working on some equipment in the back and can't be taken away from it. Docking procedure or something; preparation for lift-off. We want to keep that condition quiet for now; we can worry about Green later. How's his complexion? His breathing is a little bit rocky down here."

"It's pretty grey."

"Well, watch him but not too closely. You've got to concentrate on the immediate things, the rest can fall into place later. Don't get diverted, Feuer."

"I won't," he says and leans back, toys with the headset, groans absently. "I'll concentrate." He finds himself thinking in an abstracted way about fuckday, which is most certainly in progress right this moment, all in honor of him, when you come right down to it, and he is not sure whether he approves of the condition or feels the

90

reverse: part of it has to do with his puritan background, of course, and part has to do with the fact that he is himself, because of scruples, fear or lack of wedlock, a virgin, but looking out at the pit of Ganymede he thinks about the limbs of a woman and how her flesh, on earth, would darken toward the shades of night as he reached probing toward her breast, a sensor in the darkness, a sweeping signal in the void.

Green stirs but does not awaken.

On Mars: "Come on," Eddie says to the girl, this stinking bitch who he has been trying to make for two months now, the hell with her but he cannot stand to drop it after having so much invested. "I tell you, it's all right. It's the normal thing. Come here."

She huddles over on her side of the sandcar, an elbow draped near the window post, her eyes showing the high, frightened panic which he has come to associate with so many of the damn bitches; then the fact was that she too is a virgin and if the irony of the situation, the unmasking of the cock-teasing bitch, were not so disastrous under the circumstances and he so needful, he would find it almost funny. "Look at that," he says, pointing to the viewscreen which is now showing two popular entertainers, the focus of millions of dreams, tangled with one another in a pornographic posture underneath the lights. *Fuckday, fuckday,* a chorus is singing and the performers moan and grunt at one another as they swing to bite the mutual genitals. "Everybody's doing it," he says. "See? It's perfectly legal and like that. Every time we make a landing—"

"No, Eddie," she says in a bleating voice he has never heard from her before; usually it is very low and husky, contrived as the rest of her. "I tell you; I don't want to do it. I understand the tradition and all like that, and I know it's okay. But something in me doesn't want to do it."

"Listen," he says, pointing at the screen, then in a stab of irritation turning it off because, really, it is all the same old stuff and doesn't mean a thing to him, not when he has a chance of getting the real thing himself, "listen, it's fuckday. It's not only allowed, it's required." He would like to either beat the hell out of her and take her by force or better yet, simply throw her out of the goddamned car and let her turn blue in the sun. She is not an adapted type, she would never be able to make it back to the colony herself. "Can't you understand that? When you say you won't do it you're breaking the law or something like that. It's all legal."

"I know what it is," she says. "I heard it and heard it and I read all the things about it too. And I've been watching television and listening to you and so on but just because it's fuckday doesn't mean that all of a sudden I have to do it. I told you, anything you want you have above the waist. That part's all right. But below——"

"Damn you," he says, "we landed on *Ganymede*, don't you dig that? Ganymede! Three years ahead of the schedule. We weren't supposed to make it this shot and we did. We did. They landed safely in a crater and they're in there right now. Don't you want them to get *out*? Don't you want to show your *respect*?"

"I know," she says and sighs and twists herself somehow and then he perceives—oh, goddamn it—that the silly bitch is crying—"I know, I know it's permitted and that I'm not being very nice to anyone. But I just can't. It isn't because of you and it isn't because they made it. But I don't want to. Somehow, I never done it before."

"Then why did you come over that way?"

"I couldn't help it," she says. "I didn't want you to think there was anything different about me, that was all. Please, Eddie, let's go back. I'll do anything for you some other time, if you want to get married, but I just can't. Please, I'll never ask you anything again. Please, don't make me. I'll apologize to you and never see you if you want that. I'll even use my hands. But——"

He leans toward the wheel, puts on the ignition and races the motor. He feels himself poised, of course, between the two alternatives; he can probably rape her for one thing and by combining his strength against her guilt can prevail, but the aftermath, Ganymede or no, fuckday or not, would be difficult; the only other sensible alternative is to throw her out of the car, but he does not really want to contend with that either. It will be very bad for morale. Even though he had a right and can prove it. The fact is, he knows, that he will take her home. There is nothing else that he was ever meant to do: take the girl out, get shafted, and bring her home nicely. It is all a question of his luck, of course, but he is no virgin (not for three months now; three months and six days), he should have known better, had no reason, unless he wanted to get shafted, to take this tight bitch out on fuckday instead of almost anyone else. So in the last analysis, as always, he, Eddie, will have to pay the price.

What a bitch. "The *hell* with it," he says with a petulance which surprises him (what is she supposed to do? apologize for hurting him and say that now that she sees his point she'll blow him) and then gets the car moving, meanwhile putting on the viewscreen so that all the way back they can listen to the explorer on Ganymede exchange quips with the President on Earth, all of this intercutting between the fuckscenes; he wonders once again, as he has wondered so very often, whether he will ever see open blackness like the heroes or whether, for the likes of people like him, fuckday is as close as he will ever get to the sensation of exploration. He wonders what this astronaut, Feuer, would have done in a similar situation. Probably he would have skewered the bitch in the back seat with a single thrust and sent his hands all over and through her, knowing her in a way as profoundly as the astronaut now knows the shell of Ganymede, drifting in its tight orbit high above the gases of Jupiter, the wound of Deimos, deep in the vault of sky.

On Earth: The President, lying naked in bed next to a similarly naked woman, flips on the switch and says, "Commander Feuer? This is the President here." The woman whinnies deep in her throat at this and runs her hands once again up his thighs; they meet in an arc at his genitals and, all instinctive, he thrusts. "Cut that out," he says to her and with a slight pout she does so, her nipples retracting too in what, for her, must be a fit of petulance.

It is all in the line of things he must put up with: she is, on her own terms, an excellent lay.

"Cut what out?" he hears Feuer say thinly and the woman giggles; everything seems to be infused, at that moment, for him, with scatology, but then, this too is perfectly justifiable: it is, after all, fuckday, even for the President, mostly for his mistress. Only poor Feuer is excluded and with a rush of sympathy for the poor virginal (he has all the facts) bastard he says, "Congratulations. We're all very thrilled and happy."

"Are you, Mr. President?"

"Indeed, we are. You know what it means to us to finally have the approach to Jupiter mapped out. It *is* Jupiter, isn't it? I always get that and Saturn mixed up, but I'm pretty sure that Ganymede is Jupiter. And now that we've conquered that, we can—"

"It's not really an approach, Mr. President," Feuer says. "Actually, the whole technology hasn't been figured out yet; it's too tough down there for any of our metals—"

"Well," the President says, "well, of course, that's understood, but it's still the principle of the thing. Anyway, I just wanted to call and congratulate you, the two of you. It's a fantastic accomplishment and I'm sure that down here we're all terribly moved on your behalf. And proud and happy and celebrating. How is it, Mr. Green?"

"Green is in the back, working with some of the resonators, Mr. President. I'm afraid that he can't be disturbed, not right at this moment."

"Well, surely," the President says and grimaces as he becomes aware of what his mistress is doing to his thighs, a very peculiar balancing gesture composed of agony and pleasure by turns, it leaves him momentarily confused and shaken. "Well, of course. In any event, I simply had the same message for him. This opens up half the universe, you know."

"Half the solar system."

"Solar system, universe, what's the difference, Commander; it's all *space* and we've got it now. We've got the whole thing by the throat! Well, I guess that we won't be taking up any more of your time but we'll all be looking forward to meeting you here, just as soon as you're safely back, and in the meantime you know what's going on here. For you. In your honor," the President says with a giggle and thumbs off the speaker. Say no more, it is all inferred. He puts the telephone away and feels himself instantly absorbed in her flesh, her breasts—there would seem to be at least ten of them although this is only a significance which possesses him, not a multiplication—are all around his head, his arms, pillowing him, absorbing him, and he drinks deeply of her, biting on the nipples, thinking that he too, the President, the President no less of the entire country, he too can be humble about fuckday: wonderful fuckday, marvelous fuckday which justifies almost all of the wonderful things about this country, to say nothing of the expanse and achievements of the program and as marvelously restored he rises to poise above her once again he reminds himself that he must give Feuer and Green a citation, yes, give one to the whole program for giving this gift to the country, a gift so profound, if so mortal, in all of its implications as to justify everything that they have done. For the nation. For him. His mistress sobs, wrenches him in and he begins to fuck upon her, feeling the machinery of engorgement drive him through to the strange, beautiful connection he is making, as far as Ganymede, as mad as an escaped rocket, as profound as exploration as he dives toward completion within her.

It is really a shame that his wife knows all about his mistress, has sanctioned it for years and years. Otherwise it would top his pleasure to spring it on her today of all days. There is nothing, after all, that she can do about it. Even a President can use some extrinsic aid.

Much later, in their contentment, all the charge driven from him, all peace in the room, the whore turns to Sanders and says, "This is the sixth fuckday, isn't it? I mean, I should know these things but I keep on forgetting. I wish I had an education."

"That's right," Sanders says, all difficulties removed, only grooving with it now and this wonderful gift: all his, all his for twelve more hours and what was that he was so apprehensive about? "They teach you that crap in school.

There was Mars, Venus, Deimos, Phobos and now Ganymede. I think maybe year after next we'll have one for Jupiter. Or Titan. That's a moon of Saturn, I understand."

"What happened to the moon?" the whore says and touches her breast, once again introduces it into his mouth which forces him to mumble what he says next before he plunges into her again.

"Oh the moon," he grunts, "the moon, they weren't so advanced then, the poor bastards, they didn't know what space was good *for*. But later on it all worked out fine. Of course it didn't get formalized until recently."

"I love you," the whore says and in that moment Sanders knows she does and that he loves her too: love all of them, love all together, love progressive and unwinding, a ribbon of love which extends, flowing, from Ganymede to all of the cities of Earth and which they can ride, this one time, all the way toward their own culmination—

This treasured gift, this blessing, this permissible connection, this bestowal upon them by a gifted society: this treasured little piece of ground—

This fuckday!

X

THE MARTIAN CAMPAIGN, 2124

For four days, the dead nun lay under the barbed wire in a cold luminescence that seemed to be candlelight. In a stricken way, she seemed to be at peace, she seemed to have located an answer.

Hawkins was himself obsessed with answers during that period and he passed her twice each day, admiring the way she had taken to death, the cold frieze of her features under the stars, the slight, stony chasms of her cheek coming out against the wide brown eyes. Someone, probably a detail sergeant, had clasped her hands over the chest when she died and so there was a curious air of grace and receptivity to her aspect; almost, Hawkins thought, as if she were clutching the lover, Death, to herself past that abandoned moment when he had slammed into her. His reactions to the nun comprised the most profound religious experiences of his life.

She lay there for four days, she did, and might have been there a week if Hawkins had not taken up the issue himself with the company chaplain, insisting that something be done because such superstitious and unsettling events could turn the platoon under his command into demoralized savages.

(The chaplain, head of the corpse detail, carried a large cane and believed in the power of the cane to raise the dead and create spells. He was also sure that they were at the very point of locating the enemy and any moment, would be engaging him, finally, in actual fire.)

The next morning, when Hawkins took his men out on a patrol, the nun was gone and the barbed wire with her. In her place they had put a small block of wood on the fields; it gave her name and dates of birth and death and said something in Latin about being in memoriam. Hawkins felt much better, but later, implications of the way the nun had looked when she was dead kept on popping up in his thoughts and he decided that he didn't feel so well after all. The aliens were certainly hell to locate, they were all right at killing nuns, which was about their speed, but you simply couldn't do *battle* with them.

SISTER ALICE ROSEMARIE, etc., etc., the wood said, GONE TO HER REST 2124. BORN SOMETIME AROUND 2100 WE THINK.
IN QUONIBUS EST HONORARIUM DE PLUMS AU CEROTORIUM MORATORIUM
CAVEAT EMPTOR.

The nuns were always there during that time on Mars, administering comfort to the men and helping the chaplain out at services and even occasionally pitching in on the messline, although the men could have done without that part of it quite nicely. Someone in the company who was Catholic said that it was one of the most astonishing displays of solidarity with battle that the Church had ever given anyone. Hawkins imagined that the nuns, like himself, were simply moving around on assignments. When their orders came through, they would get out.

The nun who had been killed had, apparently, wandered out for some private religious ritual and had met stray silver wisps of the intruder's gas, which travelled from the alveoli of the lungs to become exploding emboli in the toiling blood of the ventricles, leaving her outward appearance unchanged. The other nuns, Hawkins supposed, had wanted to pick her up, but feared to defy the hastily erected signs saying AUTHORIZED PERSONNEL ONLY PERMITTED INTO THE KILLING AREA and that led to the whole complication of trying to get rid of the body. All of it still would not have been so particularly distressing to him if these events had not come in during his period of religious revival.

He had never been much for religion: men who

became captains of reconnaissance patrols in major actions were not, after all, profoundly religious types. They did what they were expected to do, that was their function and the religion, such as it was, came after the fact. Or at least that was the way that Hawkins had rationalized the thing to himself. But he had begun to feel twinges of remorse and fear from the moment that they had landed on Mars—probably helped along by all the documentary materials they had had to read on the way out about the invaders and their miraculous gift of invisibility and attack-through-subversion—and now could see that he was moving into what could be called a Second Religious Period. Just as the government had warned, there was no way of getting hold of the aliens. They were always out of sight, just behind one installation or the other. You had to be cunning.

Then too he became more and more aware of the death rate, to say nothing of the fact that the aliens—well, *something*—wanted to kill all of mankind and he began to feel convulsions, succumb to dim, vague fits of gloom in which he visualized himself taking careful vows of withdrawal. It had some subtly demoralizing effect upon his work. Still, he might have reached some fragile accommodation if it had not been for the business of the dead nun which coalesced all his thinking and began to lead him to the dismal conclusion that he was probably going insane. It had been bound to happen.

On the sixth night after the removal of the body and the erection of the wooden block, Hawkins cleaned up after he had returned to the area and in what was the best approximation of dress uniform he could manage in the terrain, wandered to the rear where the nuns were; stood idly outside the huts for a time, holding his helmet in his hands and wondering exactly what he was going to do.

Remember, they had been instructed, *the fate of all space will hinge upon your showing out here but do not feel in any way that you are under pressure. So what if we can't have a colony on Mars?*

The old nun's face seemed strangely dull and full. It passed from one of the huts toward another and then, for some reason, stopped and asked Hawkins what he was up to.

"I want to pay my respects to the dead one. To the dead . . ." In his embarrassment, Hawkins was unable to think of the word. "To the dead female priest," he said finally.

"That would be Teresa," the nun said. "She never understood what was happening out here—she always talked of birds and trees, but she had wanted to come so badly because it was the decision of the order that all of us were to come without exceptions. She said she was afraid, but all things would be part of Heaven if they deserved so and then of course she died. You were the one who arranged for her removal?"

"I suppose so," Hawkins said. "I mean, I didn't want to talk about it or anything. It's just that I wanted to pay some respects. In the long run it doesn't make any difference, though."

The old nun touched him lightly, two fingers spread to accommodate his wrist, and then led him toward the hut. "It was quite kind of you," she said, "we wanted to send for Teresa but they wouldn't let us. They said it wasn't permitted. We had to think of how she lay there in indignity—and then you returned her to us. That was very kind."

"Well, I tried."

"We couldn't manage stone so we used wood. We had to sneak the marker in. She was very unlucky, Teresa. No luck at all. Of course, most people who believe in religion surely have that problem."

"Unlucky?" Hawkins said. He had always believed that religious people made their own luck: uneven but connected.

They were at the door of the hut now, that door being comprised of a set of burlap sacks which had been strung together, and she pushed them aside to lead him in.

"Sit down," she said, pointing at some spot in the

flickering darkness where he could sense a low-slung chair. "You'll want to talk to the Mother Superior about this."

"That wouldn't be necessary."

"It's the way we do things. But she isn't prepared yet."

"Do you think I could pray here?" Hawkins asked pointlessly. "Would you mind if I did that?"

"If you want to. It doesn't do much good, though, you'd be surprised. But we can give you a book."

"No books," Hawkins said. "No *books*. I want to make up all the words by myself if I can."

"Of course," the nun said and went away. Hawkins clasped his hands and began to mumble words like *Father* and *Kyrie Eleison* and *Holy Mary*, which were about all he could remember of the things he had picked up about it, but even in the murmuring stillness, with the effect given by the one candle on the shelves above him, it wouldn't quite take.

It occurred to Hawkins for the first time that he had absolutely nothing to say to God and for some reason this cheered him; if that were the case then God probably had nothing to say to him in return. And he would undoubtedly not be in the kind of trouble he was fearing. There was no question of interference from forces or people when you had no communication with them.

He thought about the dead nun, then, and for the moment it was without horror; perhaps the calm of her features had been an utter resignation rather than a lapsed attention caught by the fumes. It was possible, in fact, that she had died in knowledge, and if that were so it made this more the bearable—although not entirely so, of course.

After a while, the curtains parted again and the old nun came out. She was dressed in what Hawkins took to be a Mother Superior's outfit, and she looked very well indeed. He was not surprised in the least; that was the way the Catholics were. He had expected this from the start.

"So then," she said. "Now I am Mother Florence and I am prepared to sit properly by you. That was a very fine thing you did for us and I'm sure that you are blessed for it."

"But why did you come out here?" Hawkins said.

He was being matter-of-fact about the identity question because it was, to be sure, the Mother Superior's business and not his. Probably, it was the Church's business. "I understand why we're out here; the government told us there are aliens to fight and it keeps us busy. But that doesn't explain you."

"We in this order believe that the revelations of Saint John are most fully realized or to be realized in the events of these particular days. We wish to hold out, for you, against the Apocalypse. It is far more likely to occur here than anywhere on Earth."

"There are no revelations of Saint John," said Hawkins, the refutation the more intense because he was not sure what he was talking about. "I don't believe there's any Apocalypse either, at least in the sense which you expect it. There's an Apocalypse every day but that's something different."

"We feel otherwise," she said calmly.

"What about your Teresa? Surely she chose to believe but dead nuns are deader than dead men. I'm sorry. There was no need for that, quite. But it's true, you know."

The nun touched his shoulder. "We have borne worse," she said. "We come and we observe; we hold and we pray. And we give what comfort we are able? What's the difference? It all works out the same way in the long run, it can keep us busy."

Later, away from the hut, Hawkins wandered toward the center of the encampment, wearing only a mask, enjoying the feeling, as he always did without proper travelling garb, that his body was going to burst from the inside. Drifting around him were strange night odors and within him his rage, and he guessed, as he picked up his pace, that when the two of them combined—the outside and the inside—they might make a kind of sense; there might be something to his feelings, his being. And in that hope he burst free, still moving, through the area itself and out to the other end, to the fields. Unswerving, poised with the grace of insistence, he plunged toward the wooden block in the distance.

When he got there, he caved it over with a sigh, feeling its edges rolling against him. He pivoted on his back, in the ease of exhaustion then, pivoted to look at the sky, wondering from where and from when and in what way his brothers the aliens would place their special silver stake in his heart.

XI

TOUCHING VENUS, 1999

Somewhere between the static and his groans he thinks that he can hear them breathing, twenty of them, two hundred, twenty thousand, it hardly makes much difference, the point is that back on earth it is the same old business as usual: respiration and expiration, sweat and death, for all the effect he has had on these mild processes he might as well have been in bed somewhere in Ohio or better yet at the space center, but he is not a contemplative man, does like this tendency for self-indulgent rhetoric which has only so recently come on him and so he pushes it away, takes a deep breath of foul, refiltered air, and puts his lips against the mouthpiece in his helmet.

"Well," he says, "well, man enters Venus, that pearl of planets, that beauty of the night-washed sky, and in so doing, he helps to open a new era of exploration, peace and progress." There is something else and for a moment he feels himself scurrying frantically for it, but then it comes and with a sense of relief so enormous that it makes him gasp, he adds, "We claim this planet for no one nation or interest but only in the name of man."

He thinks that he can hear cheering and for a moment decides that this is only another of those illusions, but no, no, it is definitely so, thirty million miles away men are roaring in the center, and for all he knows, all over the world, and then Forbes comes on, offhand, trying to keep the excitement out of his voice, but for the first time doing a bad job of it, and says, "sounding good, A-O. Sounding good." He has always been addressed as *A-O;* this is part of the new and necessary government policy of depersonalization which has reached its fruition in this new conquest. "All signals check and go. Looking tight. How is it up there anyway?"

"Well," he says and has to lick his lips, some sudden exhalation of breath has caught him flat, and he breathes in deeply, evenly, trying not to gasp, "Well, it's kind of hard to describe. It's real beautiful, but not the kind of beauty you'd associate with anything you'd know on Earth. It's kind of like a muddy, gaseous swamp, spread out as far as the eye can see; the colors are not like any swamp you'd know though, being a kind of purple and brown. Actually," he says, "actually, it's a kind of stunning beauty when you look at it in the right terms," thinking to himself that it is nothing of the sort, it is something entirely different, but there is no way in which he, much less the rest of them, can touch this: no, he will go on, the sound of his tiny, wavering voice penetrating the cosmos until he has said all they want him to say. "It's a real pleasure to be here," he finds himself adding irrelevantly, but then again they want to know that he is happy. "It's quite an unusual experience."

"Pleasure to have put you there, A-O," Forbes says. "We're all pretty excited here too, you wouldn't believe the scene. A lot of grown men are leaping. Well, have you got the markets and so on ready to plant?"

"Check," he says. The two pillars have been beside him, already they are beginning to sink into the ooze with astonishing rapidity. It is not precisely quicksand on this planet of Venus, but more like a kind of aimless, devouring slop, but there is no video on this maiden voyage, fortunately, and hence he has decided not to tell them of the seriousness of the pillar situation.

It was difficult enough getting them out of the capsule; a fifteen-minute struggle interspersed with speckles of obscenity so casual and yet so stunning in their effect that Forbes had had to say "watch it A-O" and remind him that he had already been cut off the transmission because of this. "We've told them that it's mechanical difficulties," Forbes had said, "but if you keep this up, those difficulties are going to be permanent. Now, are you going to get hold of yourself A-O or aren't you?" and he had gotten hold of himself (shit, *they* had wanted the pillars planted; he had nothing to do with that nonsense at all, and if he had to do their work he was entitled, at least, to do it in his own way), but looking now at the goddamned pillars, one of them containing a quatrain by a famous poet whose wife is a relative of the head of the agency and another an inscription supposedly thought up by the President, he wonders if it is really worth it: have they sent him thirty million miles toward the sun only as an errand boy? He does not want to think along those lines—his whole life has been dedicated, he knows, to the absence of speculation, the amelioration of thought—but now he is not sure. "Right here, Forbes," he says. "I'm placing them now, one to the left of me, about four feet from the outer edges of what appears to be a bog, the other one I'm taking right now about twenty yards down range, so I hope my voice is holding up for you while I struggle."

The fact is that he is doing nothing. There is no way in which they can verify whether or not he has done the job and future expeditions, if they find the pillars at all, will put their placement down to escape fire. As a matter of fact, there is a good chance that his escape fire will obliterate them anyway. "And there they are," he says after a short pause. "Just where they're supposed to be. Do you want me to read them now?"

"Not necessarily," Forbes says. "That's all right. We have the complete textual transcription already cleared and the poet has himself read the work."

"The quatrain is really kind of interesting," he says. "I wouldn't mind reading it from Venus if you'd like."

"We have a caller for you," Forbes says.

"Oh," the astronaut says. "How nice. To get a call up here. But hold that for a moment, I do want to read the poem. It's quite nice. *From mother earth we spun away/ into the glancing void/ and now on Venus man rests thankfully/ by this great journey buoyed.* Isn't that fine? Isn't that really excellent?"

"Check," Forbes says, withdrawing as he always does when the situation, however tentatively, seems to escape. "Putting through your call right this moment, hold on please."

"*By this great journey buoyed,*" the astronaut says

and waits for the call, figuring that it is either the President or his own wife, in neither case will it make any difference who will be coming on; they are two abstractions, too far away from Venus to induce, at this distance, any response, and so he only looks around him, up and down the range, then to the sky. He has never seen the sun on Venus until this moment, now it comes upon him with shocking force; a strange, purplish, bloated sphere which seems to move slowly across his span of vision, a suspicion of dull flames leaking from the center, the slow corona moving counterclockwise. It is a much bigger and yet somehow less deadly sun and he decides that he will describe it in due course as a purple pumpkin splitting seeds, the kind of imagery they like but then he likes it too; there is no getting around it. He grew up taking this kind of rhetoric seriously.

He wonders if Venus is inhabited. All the probes, surveys and studies have indicated that it is as desolate as Mars or the Moon, but it is a cloudy planet with several thick layers never previously penetrated, and it is not impossible that a small cabal of Venusians, after a while, might not trudge over the horizon, looking toward him. He will be asked in interplanetary code what he is doing and he is not sure that he will have a satisfactory answer: to make the Venusians or even Chinese understand what he is doing will involve a set of agreed-upon references which would take too long for it to be worth it. There is a crackle in his earphones and then the President comes on, jovial as before, across this void. "A-O," he says (he too has been indoctrinated in the rhetoric of depersonalization), "A-O, how are you? On behalf of all the peoples of the free world, I want to say that we're most grateful and—"

"I'm all right," he says. One thing at a time. "It's a strange, muddy, gaseous swamp, this Venus."

"Yes, yes, I heard that. It must be quite something up there. All of your fellow citizens—"

"The sun is purple and inflated like a balloon but lacking three dimensions, the customary three dimensions. And the sand really sucks at you; it's like mud, but only drier."

"It sounds fascinating. Just fascinating the way that you put it. All of the free and freed nations—"

"I can't really say I like it," the astronaut says, pursuing this line of dialogue for a while, although he is not sure to exactly what effect. "Of course, there's no reason why I should. You probably wouldn't be crazy about it either. Otherwise, I figure you'd be up here with me. Or maybe you'd be up here *instead* of me, come to think of it."

He hears the President chuckle; there seems to be an impression of voices behind the static and then he says, "Well, I'd give anything to be up there but I'm not, am I? I don't think that I'd have been able to have passed the very tough and testing examinations even forty years ago when I was in your age range, son. It takes a man, a most exceptional kind of man I ought to add—"

"Not really," he says, cutting him off again. This is an oddly satisfying pursuit he has discovered and he wonders why none of the others, to say nothing of himself, ever thought of it before. Having the upper hand in a discussion of this sort, it turns out, is only a matter of attitude. "It doesn't take any kind of a man at all. As long as you can retain a program but say what they want you to say and do what they tell you to do with some suggestion of initiative, you make out fine. Of course you've got to keep your blood pressure readings good but that's about the whole of it."

"Well, yes," the President says and emits what at this distance seems to be some kind of a ghastly chuckle, or is it a shudder? "Yes, of course, but on behalf of all free men everywhere—" He seems to be in something of a groove, this President and the astronaut idly wonders whether this sort of thing is difficult; certainly it is hard to do with good will. "I think that all free and freed men everywhere would—"

"Frankly," the astronaut says, "frankly I don't see the freedom. I'll be damned if you do either, you get all the hypocrisy to one side. We lost three men on Mars for no reason other than unwarranted acceleration of this foolish project, we put billions of dollars into this capsule to land one man on Venus without even clearing up the Mars mystery, and for all the effect that this is going to have on the common lives of anybody except politicians and manufacturers, it might as well not be done. Not to be offensive of course, but I did want to raise that little point.

"Come on, A-O," Forbes says. "Now come on, man."

"Come on yourself, Forbes. I've been listening to you up here on my own for two weeks. Now it's my turn. What do you think I am, anyway? How much of this do you expect a man to put up with?"

"The excitement," he hears Forbes saying. "It's the tension and the excitement, sir, that's all it is. It's quite an experience he's had and the question of isolation, well, maybe there should have been another man, but we just didn't feel then that—"

"Hey Forbes," he says and then decides to turn it into a question, meanwhile, his shoes slip and slide suddenly in the mud, and with a merry thump he falls in his spacesuit, feeling even through these layers a sensation of dim impact, waste, loss, and he rolls and rolls, trying to get up, and all the time speaking because if there is one thing you must do it is to keep the inexhaustible voice going; God forbid you should shut up and make them think of the cosmos, "Say Forbes, do me a big favor, will you? I mean, I'd take it as a personal favor and there is no doubt about it. Fuck off, will you? There's just no point to it any more. No future. I don't get it myself, personally; there's very little follow-through if you know what I'm saying."

There is no reply to this and that is all right with him, at least for the moment, because he is having increasing trouble raising himself from the mud and, instead, submits for an instant to a feeling of panic; the suit is incorrectly balanced, his motions too frantic, the mud too absorbing, and he thinks that he will never be able to get up and will become an artifact like the pillars, but after a while he forces himself to think this whole thing through logically and then, placing one limb before the other in a consciously rationalized progression, is able to come to his feet, after all. It has been a terrifying experience which strips him, at least momentarily, of the more metaphysical concerns involved in his conversation with the President and he finds that he is sweating heavily. On Venus. "Son of a bitch," he says. "Son of a bitch; son of a bitch, the whole damn thing is crazy. They got no idea, not one of them, of what's really going on here. I might have died."

"No such luck," Forbes says with some crispness. He seems to have assumed a new mode; now he is adopting that one with which, some time ago, he had so expertly directed the triggering of the computer for the landing. It is not a tone reserved for disputation. "No such at all. We cut you off, Williams. It's just you and me now and the monitors. We were able to catch every single one of your foul-mouthed obscenities on the lag and announce that it was technical troubles. Do you really think we wouldn't have had a lag built in? Right now the President is giving you a medal because of the unfortunate breakdown in communication. You never had a chance with your disgusting little plan, you see, and you'll never have one again. We have our ways. We have methods."

"I had no plan."

"You had it worked out from the beginning, you bastard; you probably decided on this ten years ago and you thought that it would sneak through your disgusting liberal charade, but it's too late, A-O, you can't do that any more. We've got our methods, you know."

"Can I talk to my wife?" he asks. "I understand that she's there."

"No, I don't think so. And I don't think your wife can talk to you. Do you know what we're going to do when you get back?" Forbes says. "We're going to put you in a boat and take you undersea to California and when we get you there, we'll throw you in a cell for the rest of your life and announce that you've had a breakdown. You're finished, A-O. You'd be better off on Venus but no such luck because you are coming back."

"I never liked her that much anyway," the astronaut says. "She never understood my problems. She thought that the whole thing was just so that she could get her

110

recipes in the newspapers. Actually, I don't think I want to talk to my wife at all, it was just a whim. No, I'll stick it out here."

"No you won't."

"The hell I won't," the astronaut says and shrugs, an enormous lifting shrug which is intended to induce, at long-distance, a mood of renunciation, but strangely the gesture for once becomes the affectation and he finds that he feels very careless suddenly, very free. Never in his whole life has he seen things so clearly as he does at this moment; even his wife, for once, would agree that he is being strictly logical. "The thing is that I'll be free. I'm not coming back. I'll be free on Venus."

"Free on Venus," he repeats and with a mad, merry laugh pushes the switch that will shut off the transmitter. Now, in deep Venusian silence, he trudges over to the pillars, upsets them, presses with a heel into the mud and stands, for an instant, looking toward the craft. He cannot decide whether he will dismantle it or not; perhaps the best thing would be an unmonitored launch which will send him shrieking toward the heavens, poised in outer orbit; then he can head the ship toward the sun, raving all the way. (He knows that it is perfectly impossible for him to remain on Venus; the computer is programmed to trigger at a given time and take the support systems with it.) On the other hand, perhaps he could end it all here. It docs not matter: hc has plenty of time. There is no little satisfaction in this. He has never had time before. He has never known what it was like.

The receiver in his helmet crackles thinly and Forbes says, "Don't try to turn me off, A-O. We have an emergency override, you know. Now get into that ship and get ready for countdown. We're doing a partial abort and we're bringing you home right now."

"No I won't. I won't do it. You can't make me."

"No we can't," Forbes says. "But you'll make yourself. You want to be a hero, don't you? You want to be an American hero, not some stinking alien piece of scum festering on Venus. We'll make you a hero, A-O. No matter what happens to you, we wouldn't spoil that. Now get back into that fucking ship you son of a bitch and cut the chickenshit. You're part of the combine, just like everybody else. You're no different. Who the hell gave you the idea that you were any different?"

The astronaut thinks about this for a moment. He looks at the bloated sun while all the facts of his existence seem to tumble through him, being sorted out, working toward some kind of balance, and then he has his final insight. It is one so vast as to render insignificant everything else which he has thought today and in the weeks previous. It simultaneously ends and begins everything.

"You want to be a hero, don't you?" he hears Forbes say, but this is really irrelevant. "All your life you were trained to be a hero, you won't stop now because you had a little blowup, will you? Of course you won't, A-O, you don't know anything else."

"Well yes," he says with some deliberation, "well yes, I see now. You're perfectly correct."

And stumbles back to the ship and up the ladder and into the depressurization cabin and after a time into the main cabin itself where, sitting in his underwear, humming thinly, drumming his fingers on the plastic, he prepares for liftoff and the magnificent reception that he knows most surely awaits him.

XII

THE MESSAGE ON DEIMOS, 2309

Deimos and Phobos were artificial satellites, of course, constructed by the Martians a long, long time ago to provide them with heat and light and air in the face of a dying technology and ecological balance. They hung around doing their job for a long time, but like most machines, after a while, they broke down and then, after a while, so did Mars. For what they were, however, they worked very well, as based upon our estimates that the Martians were able to survive for some ten thousand years after the moons were launched. That would have meant that they hung on until shortly before the beginning of our Dark Ages, which is an interesting irony when you come to think of it, our Dark Ages and the end of the Martians coming at about the same time. It makes you think about symmetry. Kathy and I went over to Phobos yesterday to read the tablets. That's the craze now, you know.

Everybody is reading the tablets on Phobos. The full text of the writings has been released in several editions on Earth (it is in the public domain so that this makes it very easy to do), several cults have been founded about these writings and the first of the tourist excursions is figured to begin almost any time at all, maybe next month. For the first time in almost a hundred years, Mars looks as if it will become something of an industry again. It's about time. Life here in the colony has been progressively dull and it is hard to shake the feeling (the feeling up until the last few months, I mean) that if some monumental disaster were to occur here the news would be at least three hours getting to Earth and it would be months and months before they sent anyone to pick up the pieces. And then, they'd do it grudgingly.

It hadn't held up too well, in short, and the new interest in the tablets is long overdue, the thing that may turn the entire Mars project around. In the meantime, those of us on the skeleton crew who are up here are now making hay, putting our memoirs together and etc., getting good snapshots of the blasted terrain so that we can show exactly what happened to this planet, some of us even hooking into the cults as local emissaries. There are three distinct cults, you know. There are the Phobists who believe that the writings are sacred and a terrible bit of warning and prophecy to mankind, the demi-Phobists who believe that what happened was a kind of deliberate sacrifice on the part of God so that Earth would live (there is only so much life permitted in one solar system at a given time) meaning that we owe to the divine an almost mystical sense of humility plus a pledge never to, by reason of sin, permit ourselves to be in an equivalent situation some day and the Basilicans who believe that the writings extracted from Phobos are a hoax, planted there by human ancestors who, in the time of Atlantis, were space travelers and who launched the whole plot in an effort to frighten future travelers from other empires into leaving Atlantis alone. (Why they wanted to be left alone and how they were able to have space-flight from Atlantis I do not know, but here on Mars we are very far from what is new and interesting on Earth and must do as well as we can with pre-digested supplements, recorded news and our own assumptions.) For some reason, it would appear that the Basilicans (I do not understand why they have given themselves or been given this name) are considered anti-religious while the Phobists and demi-Phobists are aligned with a resurgence of Fundamentalism.

So it is only a matter of time now until the leaders of the various cults, plus followers, curiosity-seekers, the jaded and the anti-religious come up here to approach the root source of the mysticism, so to speak. When they do—and as we understand it, the first formal expeditions will begin by the end of next month—we are all likely here in the colony to be in a strong or stronger position, but none stronger than Kathy or myself, who are the only people to have been privy to the thoughts and reactions of Hays, the discoverer of the tablets, after he found the writings. In his excitement, scrambling around the abandoned satellite after the revelation of the tablets, he forgot to make certain adjustments in his oxygen feed and carbon-dioxide expulsion and died quite hideously some twelve hours later. Before he did, however, we, his closest friends in the colony, were at his bedside during the last moments. He wasn't very happy about the whole thing, I might note.

Not just the question of his dying, with which he could deal most comfortably. The majority of us here on Mars have adjusted to the question of our ongoing death a long time ago or we could not be here. Hays had been more suicidal than most, his reason for applying for the colony in the first place had been that his fourth wife left him, exactly as the first three had, and he felt that he was falling deep into a pattern of unreconstruction where he could see the rest of his life fully mapped out for him and he did not like it. "I don't mind the fact that I can't seem to get along with women," he had said to us once, "because all things being equal, there's no particular reason why anyone should, what gets me is the fact that I seem bound, over and over again, to trying to prove I *can* and that indicates that to a certain degree I haven't faced reality. I was very romantic about all four of the bitches too, I believed that it was possible to construct meaningful relationships and so on." What concerned Hays most in his final hours was the question of the tablets themselves. He was not at all convinced that his discovery would add to an increase of human knowledge.

"You see," he said (gasping out the words heavily and with much difficulty, his entire respiratory system had been wrecked and the doctors, granted their primitive technology and training, had only been able to get that he try not to talk, but as it was obvious to everyone that it was toward the end, Hays paid this little heed), "you see, they'll miss the real message of the thing all the way through and they'll just turn it into another way to make people scared. They'll say that the Martians died because of such and such reasons and therefore we must not do

115

these things or we too will die, but what they will never admit is that perhaps the Martians wanted to die, or that their actions were not related to saving them or that even the whole thing has to be judged in a way and in terms of a system of looking at things entirely different from ours. We've looked at things only in one way since we were created and that's why we'll never change and why things have worked out this way over and over again, but sooner or later we will have to understand, if there are any of us left, that we occupy only one percent of the known way of thinking and feeling and that there are other terms just as valid. I knew the minute I stumbled across these tablets that they were going to have an enormous impact and that's why I got so excited and was such a damned fool about the respirator, but they're going to work out all wrong, no one will understand the real meaning here. The real meaning is something far beyond us, we have to struggle and try to find out what it is. Why did they put the preservative equipment in *satellites?* They could have done it just as well on Mars itself, what was the reason that they had to fling it into orbit, thousands and thousands of miles from where anyone could *reach* it? Was the reason this: that there was something as profoundly destructive in them as there was in us and they could not trust themselves not to destroy the apparatus? Or was the work of preservation done by an underground who resisted the efforts of the government to let the plant die, and had to put the project way out in space to protect it? We will have to think of these things, think of them long and intimately," Hays gasped and then he died while Kathy and I leaned over him, taking all of this in, all of the implications and the suffering and most incontestably moving it was. Hays was probably the best friend we had in the colony, outside of each other that is to say, but he did not know how to take care of himself and he was stupid and that is why he died. Perhaps there is some truth to what he said. In any event, as per the wishes he had expressed, we talked to the Administrator and tried to get the discovery buried, keep the contents of the tablets and so on way out of the public domain, but he said that this would not be fair; we were all employees of the civil service and had the obligation to turn over any useful information and findings to the government promptly, also this was the only thing of some interest which had occurred on Mars for a very long time and our turning it over might give the entire project a shot in the arm. He was right about that, of course. So it went out over the wire and the tablets themselves on the next ship and to our enormous surprise it started building almost immediately. The Administrator's main worry had been that Hays's discovery of the tablets would raise questions as to why this had not been discovered a long time ago; had all of the colonists and investigators been incompetent? but strangely that never came up at all. It was taken for granted that opening a hatch near the entrance porthole, right where the network of machines began, would have been an unexpected and dangerous action and that Hays had been out of his mind to have done it. In any event, hundreds of years later, it managed to solve the Phobos mystery and the scientists were so happy to have a rationale, at last, for all those machines that the questions which might have originated with them never did. The cults took all the play away. It was amazing how quickly it started and generated steam. Of course things accelerate, go faster and faster these days. Yesterday Kathy and I went up to Phobos.

We went up to Phobos on the service boat, no problems whatsoever. Originally our intention had been simply to pay a kind of tribute to Hays before the tourists came in, a last look at the isolation before the swarm and so on, but by the time we got into docking we understood that something entirely different had been on our minds all the time; something which only then were we willing to admit to one another. We wanted to go where Hays had been. We wanted to see the place from where he had extracted the documents. We wanted to share, vicariously, the sense of power and mysticism which must have flooded through him at the moment he extracted the tablets from their hiding place and laboriously had fed them through the decoder, share the astonishment and wonder with which he must have greeted the words of the tablets as they came out to him. For better or worse, it was the most profound thing which had occurred on or near Mars for several generations and we wanted to be part of it. Also, a first-hand article by the surviving friends of the explorer on their impressions of the site would tie in nicely with the other stuff. You have to take the long view.

Amazingly (or not so amazingly; it all depends upon the way you look at it, there is a certain fine duality to all of human affairs, motives and actions) we were the first from the colony to go to Phobos since the incident itself. That would surely change and Phobos was already under government edict as a Highly Secured Area, but in the few weeks since, no one had thought to go up there. It was the same cold, still, deadly machinery floating in the strange gravitational field, the same humming and whimpering of lost circuits, the same stricken emptiness. Tablets or not, nothing had changed at all. Why bother to see it? There were more useful things to do.

We put the ship's platform into the dock and Kathy said, "What do you think we'll find? The spirits of the Martian elders come to strike us down in vengeance for unearthing their racial secrets?"

"I doubt it," I said. "I don't think that the elders would bother making it up here. They'd just take the colony out."

"Hays must have suffered terribly."

"Yes, he did," I said. "I don't think that it made any difference to him at all at the end. You get a different kind of man in the project nowadays. It used to be a more experimental type, but now too many turn out like Hays."

She put a hand on my arm and leaned close, let me smell her as she inclined the profile of her cheek, somehow pitiless and impermeable in the fluorescence of the craft, and said, "Do you want to screw first?"

"Do you?"

"I don't know. It's kind of exciting in a way but you think of all this history in back of you and you wonder."

"Let's skip it," I said. "We've done that already anyway." It's kind of a house secret, but almost everyone in the colony has done it at one time or another. It's almost mandatory to visit the satellites at least once and there, in all that isolation, the impulse to screw is irresistible. Perhaps because it is such a human thing, but somehow I doubt it.

We put on the suits and went through the dock and into Phobos. We could see a couple of pieces of Hays's gear scattered around the entrance, probably because he had left in such haste, so that part was all right. I mean, we established that it was this entrance he had taken into Phobos, just as he had said. There are a couple of other portholes, smaller areas, on the other side, but practically no one uses them any more since they don't exit into the machinery. We used the flash lights for illumination and I began looking around for signs of the hatch which Hays had pulled open. He had described it very carefully and although he had said it was concealed in a bulkhead, there was no way you could miss it once you knew where you were looking, if you listened carefully to what he had said. We had listened very carefully.

Well, of course. It figured. There was no bulkhead. There was no hatch. There were no marks. There was nothing at all, no indication. Kathy began shaking her head and after a while I did too. Then she began giggling and I found that reasonable and joined her. Then we realized together that giggling was not precisely the answer, so we stopped.

"Well," she said through the transmitter (it is strange to be standing next to a person yet need mechanical equipment to transfer the sound of speech; perhaps this has something to do with the sheer mystery of these airless satellites), "well, do you think that he made up all of that himself and just waited for the proper time to spring it?"

"It's hard to say. It might have been written by one of his ex-wives and this was his way of paying tribute to her."

"What will happen when they come up here and find that there isn't any hatch?" One thing about the kind of relationship we have developed; there is little room for equivocation or circumlocution. We think alike and we

119

think very much to the point. Occasionally we even talk that way. "Won't that establish that the whole thing was a hoax?"

"I don't think it will make the slightest bit of difference," I said. "Remember, the people observing this are going to be, most of them, affiliated with the cults. They'll find a way to cover it. No, I think that if they were ripe for this they were ripe for it, and it won't really matter at all."

"Poor people," Kathy said.

"Think of our own opportunities," I said. Then I helped her across the dock and we got into the boat and closed up the apparatus and got the hell out of there as quickly as we could. We decided on the way that if anyone in the colony asked us what it had been like up there we would go along with Hays's cover and say that it had been fine. But no one asked us. You see, the point is that no one here precisely cares.

So they are coming soon, maybe tomorrow, maybe next week. They will come to write up the first detailed accounts of life in Mars for many years, and as Hays's oldest and closest friends in the colony, Kathy and I are bound to be important interviewees.

My only question then at the present moment in time is this: Should I do my memoirs with particular reference to interpretation of the precious tablets (my basic specialty after all is linguistics) or should I concentrate upon a biography of Hays the prophet?

Both are quite tempting, but Kathy thinks that the life of the biography may be longer. I think so too, but as a question of personal vanity, have always wanted a book of my own life available and might be willing to sacrifice the more crass commercial benefits in order to make a gesture of some personal integrity. Kathy thinks personal integrity be damned; it is time to go back to Earth and try to live, once again, the semblance of a normal life.

AFTER TITAN, 2500+

The juggler grins. Flicks the clubs from one hand to the next. Orange, yellow, dim flashes of light. Quick movement then; dim impact of sky to the frozen Earth. The last; the last. The last juggler. Come to the night after the storm.

It is very dark.

They watch. Six of them, eight of them on the bare fields before the stand. Watching the juggler. What unusual intentness! but this of course, is the last time. Afterward, the trapeze, the lions. Perhaps a sword eaten or vomited whole. Finally, the elephants. But first ... first the juggler. In the night he prances a little. The last night. The last prance.

"Come," he says to the two who are with him. "Come closer. Watch the juggler juggle. Later, we'll take his hand."

The two say nothing—solemn little girls in pastel dresses (dreams?), lollipops dangling like unheeded cigarettes from their mouths. Recently they have seen so much. Fires. Disease. Other problems. Now a juggler. It is all a strain. They are six and eight. Eight and six. Difficult ages. Difficult times.

"We'll miss it," the boy says, "if we don't go now." He tugs at their hands. There is always the possibility that the juggler will sign his name. In the sand, on a sheet of paper. Who knows? It is all terrribly significant. The boy is ten. A significant age. Critical happenings.

"And now," says the juggler on the parapet. "Now, I will do my final trick. The end of juggling." He sighs, winks, tips his cap at the sky. "Watch, watch it closely now. Think about this."

He hurls four, five, six—oh, a great many!—clubs into

the air; watches them distantly, catches them, flings them one by one into the night. Mud belches, absorbs them as mud so often does. The juggler salutes the Earth.

"That is all," he says. "There is no more."

He bows, scrapes his palms. Applause is forbidden, of course. "Juggling is finished," he says. "Not a moment too soon." He nimbly jumps from the parapet, runs behind the huge tent.

"Oh," the boy says. "We won't get any autographs. He left too soon."

"Was he afraid?" Six asks.

"I don't know."

The two say nothing further, staring at the empty stage, holding their lollipops. The others wink at them . . . the others in the audience, that is. They are the only children . . . except, of course, that there are no children here at all. Not for some time.

"Watch what comes next," an old man says. He nods at the boy. "Lions. Trapezes with nets. Elephants. Isn't that nice? It's a wonderful thing that they're doing for you."

"Very nice," the boy says dutifully, but he is thinking of other things; thinking, perhaps, of the juggler who is behind the tent and who neither he nor Six and Eight will ever see again. "Stop that," he says to Six, who is scratching her palm insistently with the fingernails of the other hand. "Don't do that. You know what happens next?"

"What?"

"The hand falls off."

"Oh," says Six. She takes some gum from a pocket, slips it past the lollipop and chews.

"It turns black and then it falls off," Eight adds.

"Never mind," he says. "Stop this." He wishes to concentrate on other things, not simple teasing. Light has come up on the parapet again: a man has entered with a carrying case. He drops the case clumsily to a seat and then opens it. Two rabbits come out, dignified as only a certain kind of rabbit can be. These are the last rabbits, of course.

"Good evening," the man says. "Welcome."

Someone applauds. Remembers the Condition. Stops himself, pattering into silence.

"The last magic show," the magician says.

The rabbits peer at one another. He picks them up, holds them together, touches their noses gently. The rabbits blink, touch tongues. The Magician laughs. Apparently he has had a long relationship with these rabbits because they look at him with disapproval.

"So," he says. "Disappear."

He does something with a hand. The rabbits disappear. Suddenly they are on the other side of the parapet.

"Now watch closely," the Magician says. "This took great training and discipline. I deprived myself, personally, for years and years so that I would know how to do this well. Nothing in this profession comes easily, you know. You have to pay out an important bit of yourself in order to learn how to manipulate cunningly. What you lose you can never recover."

The rabbits, indubitably, are dancing. Their forepaws mesh; they cling, rise to a stiff posture. The Magician claps his hands. They lumber with a certain skill.

"Dancing rabbits," the Magician says. "Do you know what it takes from a rabbit to dance? Well, don't even ask. These are the last dancing rabbits. I think that they are grateful for this."

"I don't like this," Six says to the boy. "He isn't very nice. He's kind of mean."

"Now they fly," the Magician says. "Fly deep."

The two rabbits flick out, vanish; appear on the roof of the parapet in confusion, their faces drawn. They appear to be thinking the whole thing over. The Magician salutes them.

"They vanish."

They do.

"Think of the cost," the Magician says reflectively, stroking his chin. "Nothing is as simple as it looks. Action and reaction. Interdynamic complexities. The collision of possibilities, the meshing of the network of chance in the slow confusion of touch. Now I need a volunteer."

"He was cruel to the rabbits," Six says. "He didn't have to do that. I *know* where they are. They're dead."

"Oh hush," Eight says. "It's all just a trick. He doesn't have anything to say anyway, everybody knows that stuff. It's just fraud."

"Quiet," the boy says. He, on the other hand, is ten, he knows of life. Rabbits are born; rabbits die. Somewhere in between, they are likely to vanish. It is a condition of the Universe. Blame the rabbits.

"It's only a trick," he says. "You shouldn't even think about things like that if you take it seriously."

"They're dead," Six repeats, holding Eight's hand. "I know I'm right. They both died."

"It makes no difference."

"A volunteer," says the Magician. "For my next and very last trick. Brought to you direct by consignment. A volunteer."

"Not me," Six says. "He's cruel."

"Not me," says Eight. "He's silly."

Meanwhile, the others are looking at them. "You ought to go," the old man says. "One of you ought to go. I mean, this thing is for children, basically. It's not fair for us."

"They don't want to go," the boy says. "I can't make them. Why should you think I could?"

"How about you?"

"That's right," a young woman says. "It's a child's obligation. One of you has to go."

"Not me," says Eight. "Not me. I'm not a rabbit."

"A volunteer," says the Magician. His voice is higher and there seems to be a sheen on his forehead. Which makes him the only person in the world who is sweating at the present time.

The boy shrugs, raises his hand. One way, the other way. It works out the same way. He had thought of it in terms of clowns, colors leaping, flashes of costume in the sunlight. Nevertheless. What the hell. Magicians have an ancient and respectable tradition, antedating clowns by some five hundred years in the royal courts.

"I'll go," he says. "I volunteer, I mean."

The Magician looks him over carefully from the parapet. "Well," he says, "I just don't know. I mean, how about the little girls?"

"They say they won't go."

"It's only a *trick*," the Magician says petulantly. "You've got the wrong idea if you think—"

"I said I'll go," the boy says. "Why ask someone if you won't take them?"

The Magician shrugs, turns his back, seemingly thinking about this. When he turns again he has a different face ... somewhat younger with trimmed mustaches, the eyes still the same. A simple use of cosmetics. Stage technique. Very old. Very familiar. The boy knows this. "All right, son," the Magician says, "come on up then if you really want."

He pats Six on the head, tweaks Eight by the ear, touches both for luck. He passes through the others—who are, when you think about it, not very many at all, but still a better crowd than you might think under the circumstances—and hops to the stage. Close to him now, the boy finds that the Magician is drunk. A peculiar foul smell comes from his clothing, his lips. He touches the boy. Up closer he is much older in a young way; younger in an old way. It is very strange. It has to do with cosmetics.

"Don't pay any attention to it," the Magician whispers frantically. "It doesn't affect the performance."

"Pay any attention to what?"

"Do you play well at vanishing?" the Magician asks, back in performance role. "Tell me the truth now."

"Yes. Sometimes." He pauses. "I don't want to vanish though."

"Just for a little while."

"You see," he says, pointing to Six and Eight, "you see, well, they're with me." He does not know why he is embarrassed but he finds the situation suddenly very difficult to carry on and wishes that he were off the stage in dreams. Of course that would work out in the same way.

"You'll be right back. Don't worry about them, they can take care of themselves. It only takes a minute anyway."

"I don't care," the boy says. "If you want it that way, have it. I'll vanish then."

"Do you hear that?" the Magician says. "He's okay with vanishing. Vanishing is tops with him. What will things come to next?"

The boy hears some rustling behind him. Applause. The conditions then have been momentarily relaxed. High cackling sounds from in front. The Magician darts to a side, brings back a large box, places it center stage, grunting. The boy is very happy. A deep box whose cover the Magician now swings back.

"In," he says.

"Wait. What do you want?"

"Nothing," says the Magician. "I am a professional. This is a performance. The last one, but a performance nevertheless. Show some common respect for artifice, for the devices of manipulation! You don't know everything you understand." The Magician has adopted a professional manner; a professional brusqueness. He wonders if Six and Eight can see into the box. He hopes not. It is black inside with speckles of white and green.

"It's very dark in there."

"Of course it's dark. How did you think it would be? Floodlights? An orchestra?"

"It's very, *very* dark."

"When you come out, even the night is bright," the Magician says. "Now. Into the box, please."

"I don't know—"

"You're only a little boy and I am the last Magician. You must listen to me, that's the way it is. Into that box."

The boy shrugs, puts a foot delicately into the box. A dampness comes over his foot; passes up his leg.

"I don't want to go in there," the boy says.

"Don't be silly. I called for a volunteer. You came up on that basis."

"I'm not a volunteer."

"Yes you are. Once you're into it you're a volunteer. Now, get into that box."

"No."

The Magician pauses, fondles his chin and considers

the audience. "He doesn't want to go in," he says. "Is anybody out there willing to take his place?"

The boy hopes that Six or Eight will say *yes*—after all, it is only one thing or the other—but he hears nothing. After a moment, the Magician says gently, "You see now, it's hopeless. You volunteered. You're up here. There's no one else, and you have to do it on your own. Now be a brave boy and beyond that be reasonable and get into that box."

The boy shrugs. The Magician, he understands, is quite right. There is nothing else to do. He is committed: trapped in the trapped feeling in the trapped world. It makes no difference. He gets into the box.

Inside, he puts his arms at his sides, looks up at the sky. "Now, be patient," the Magician says. He leans over the box, pats the boy gently on the forehead, purses his lips in a graceful kiss. "Just relax."

The boy tries to relax.

The Magician closes the lid.

There are stars inside the box.

"The last vanishing," he hears the Magician say.

Six and Eight are fascinated. Now the last Magician has vanished the boy. How remarkable! Even if he did not really volunteer. Soon will come the last lion tamer. Then a sword swallower. (They have followed it on the program.) Then the elephants.

Finally, the elephants.

They plan to volunteer to ride them. There are ways and ways.

And ways.

XIV
THE REVOLT ON GANYMEDE 2471

THE BASIC POLITICAL SITUATION BEGINS TO CRUMBLE

Things are breaking down. That tentative alliance with which Davis and I had managed to hold Wilson in check has now disintegrated and for the first time in some weeks the basic political discord under which we live has begun to assert itself; it is apparent that, once again, there is a revolution in the wings. Wilson has begun to edge toward arrogance and caprice once again and has embarked upon a new policy which he calls 'fundamental radicalism' which can only lead to disaster if he is not checked. Nevertheless, Davis will not see the urgency of the situation. I believe that he and Wilson have, behind my back, arranged a certain pact to swing the balance of power and therefore I must take action soon. But I do not quite know in what direction to proceed. Representing the basic liberal forces on Ganymede as I do, I must be careful to see that all action is relevant, sane and constructive yet graced by assurance. I am not clear yet. I am moving toward a sense of accommodation.

Last night Wilson summoned the full council into extraordinary session. Ordinarily we meet once a week but in times of crisis it becomes the President's option. When I came to the chambers I found Davis already there, sitting in intense conference with Wilson, the two of them leaning toward one another on their elbows, talking rapidly. When they saw me they sprang apart, Davis with a peculiar glazed expression and a strange expression of guilt as he cupped his hands in front of him. Wilson lost no time in getting to the crux of the meeting, bringing the chamber into session and delivering the following speech:

"I summon this extraordinary plenary session of the Ganymede Council," he said, "because we are faced with one of the most severe crises in the history of this planet; a crisis whose very dimensions can shake us, so appalling are they. It is clear that certain dissident elements in the population, certain members of the disaffected minority have contemplated acts of sedition and sabotage against the legitimately constituted government, and although such acts have been only scattered and can be easily controlled by the enormous powers of the central government, we cannot yet dismiss the fact that we are moving into crisis. I am here therefore to request this evening that I be given the power of extraordinary option so that the duly constituted government may be able to throw its full weight behind the effort to control the seditionists and maintain a better life for all of us."

"I'll buy that," Davis said. He was sitting on Wilson's left in a posture of curious intimacy, an elbow cocked forward in a semi-contorted position, brushing against Wilson's right arm, his chin cupped in his hand. "We can't have any sedition here. It would break the back of the program. I would certainly vote for extraordinary power."

"Wait a moment," I said. "I'm not sure that I understand this. In what direction have the seditionists been functioning? What are your plans? What is the menace?"

"I'm afraid I can't go into that," Wilson said. "This is confidential information available only to the administration at the present time, to release it to the special session would be to put highly explosive material into the public domain and the national security might be menaced. As the duly elected president of Ganymede I think that I can make this judgment."

"He's perfectly correct," Daivs said. "I vote the extraordinary powers."

"Shouldn't headquarters be notified?" I asked. "It would seem that this is something of which they should be advised."

"Certainly not," Wilson said. "This is a local problem which can be handled under local jurisdiction. Besides, the seditionists have wrecked the transmitter. We haven't been able to get a message out for two days. This is part of the information I was withholding in the national interest but now must tell you."

"I don't quite know what to say," I said.

"There's very little which can be said," Wilson said. "Under the constitution, a two-thirds majority is sufficient to convey these powers and since Davis has voted in that way, your vote is not needed. Of course unanimity would be a most convincing display for the seditionists; it might break their spirit.

"I abstain," I said. That is my right. Each of us under the Constitution represents a given block of votes which we must vote not only in our own interests but in that way which we feel will best represent the constituency. Feeling that my constituency had not yet been sufficiently advised of the dimensions or nature of the danger, I voted for their sake to withhold further judgment.

"Well," Davis said, "that's it then."

"Yes it is," said Wilson. "I appreciate this vote of confidence and will do my best to bring a firm hand down upon the contraindicating elements. That concludes the business of this meeting."

"I have some things which I want to discuss privately," Davis said, giving me a meaningful look. "If you don't mind."

"I don't mind," I said and went out. I went to my own quarters and made the latest entries in my diary, being careful to record the events without prejudice and as faithfully as possible. Having been detailed without the knowledge of either Davis or Wilson to write up their performances in great precision, I wanted to get the facts of the meeting down while they were still fresh in my mind. After I had finished I went to the transmitter to check it and found that indeed it was not working at the present time. Clear evidences on the equipment indicated that it had been tampered with by person or persons unknown. I fear that an era of repression is now beginning. Wilson was elected President for this session on an essentially libertarian platform, but seems to have forgotten his campaign promises. Of course, if sedition is actually occurring on the project, he is within his rights, although the situation must be watched very carefully. I am concerned with Davis, who has seemingly neglected his responsibilities as duly elected leader of the opposition— the loser of the election automatically fills this important post—but am willing for the moment to maintain a policy of watchful waiting.

A FEW POLITICAL COMMENTS

Nothing of this sort occurred during my own administration which ruled in peace and tranquillity from hour 24900 to hour 25900 over a contented populace in an era of great expansion and hope. There were no complaints of sedition, no dissident elements, and when I stepped down it was with the gratitude of a thankful populace. The majesty of my most recent administration is not to be denied. I now understand that I probably made a mistake in not standing for election again, but under the Constitution two consecutive terms are permitted only once and I felt it best to save this important option to such time as my abilities at healing and peacemaking would be most severely needed. I did not understand that the tranquillity and progress of my administration were by my own hand and that all along I had been guiding the ship of state gracefully over troubled waters. At the time that my term did end, however, and I stepped down, I thought that Wilson was capable of carrying on satisfactorily; he had shown administrative gifts of his own during previous terms and I could not understand how things could have gotten to this pass so quickly.

I could call for impeachment, but I do not believe I have the votes, and in any event there is always the possibility that Wilson is right and the project is in great danger. In such a case, I would be no less of a seditionist than the others in trying to force a precipitate change of administrations during a period of national crisis. I must, therefore, bide my time.

THE CRISIS BUILDS

Today Davis found me in my own quarters, entering in a high state of agitation and distress. He locked the door behind him—an unusual precaution—and said that it was vital that we confer immediately. "I'm afraid of Wilson," he said. "I think that he's lost control of the situation."

It gave me a great deal of satisfaction to say, "Remember, I was the one who abstained during the last session. It was *you* who lent your vote and support to Wilson."

"Well yes," he said, "That's true. I felt that the highest loyalty was to the state itself and Wilson, since he is now the President, embodies the state. But I believe I have made a terrible mistake. He is taking a very, very hard line, a very repressive line if you want to know the truth, and I believe that the entire question of sedition is merely a red herring raised in our midst in order to conceal his own megalomania. These are hard words, a very difficult position to take. I have a sense of tragedy in saying them, but trust your confidence and feel that it must

132

be put on the line. I think that Wilson is very dangerous at the present time."

"So what do you suggest that I do?" I said. "We've never had problems like this during my administrations."

"Nor during mine," Davis said. "Nor for that matter, even with his up until the present time. It is my judgment that he cannot take pressure and the responsibility of the position, after all this time, is beginning to tell. I see very, very difficult times ahead." He leaned forward and put his mouth virtually to my ear. "I hate to say this but I suspect Wilson himself of wrecking the transmitter in order to facilitate his own reign of tyranny. Do you know how to set it up again?"

"Of course not. I'm a sociologist."

"And I'm a biochemist," Davis agreed gloomily. "Only Wilson, the technician, has the knowledge to restore the equipment, and he says at the present time that he will not do so because the revolutionaries will only wreck it again. First he wants a purge and then to re-establish communication with Headquarters. That's very dangerous thinking, don't you agree?"

"I agree," I said. In recent weeks, Davis has developed something of a nervous tic and the normal healthy pallor of his complexion has shifted to a high brightness. Perhaps it comes from being so close to the machines all the time. "Nevertheless, I have agreed to take a position of watchful waiting," I said to calm him, "and I think that you should do so as well. This would be the best advice I could give. After all, there will be a new election in only 300 hours or so and that will be time enough to get at the problem."

"But you don't follow," Davis said hoarsely. "I've been in close communication with Wilson over these days, very very close communication indeed, and I believe that it is his intention to nullify elections when they come up because of the situation. He construes our vote for extraordinary powers as approval of this should it come to a constitutional test."

"I didn't vote for extraordinary powers."

"Well, I didn't either. I mean, I had no idea that this

was the kind of thing on his mind and I certainly would not have permitted my vote to have been used in that way if I had been aware of it. Listen, I want your support."

"I don't quite understand. I told you, I think that the proper position to take now is one of watchful waiting." This had always been my policy during my administration, a low-keyed, level-headed approach to the problems on Ganymede which had won me the name and reputation of The Great Peacemaker. "If it comes to that kind of crisis, we can then assess our position."

"I don't think we can wait. There's no telling what he might do, he's out of control. I want to call an impeachment session. A full plenary. And then I want to solicit your support for the Presidency itself. I would like to run for the job."

"Well, why not me?" I said. "Granted the situation is as extraordinary as you construe it to be, which I certainly do not, but granted that, certainly the times are ripe for a peacemaker, a conciliator, a calm, level-headed Presidency which will move us out of the age of repression and into a new, quiet kind of libertarianism—"

"Not necessarily," Davis said. "I mean, I'm not disagreeing with your position or your gifts at all. Or even that you'd make an excellent President just as you have so many times already. It's just that I don't think that you can get the broad base of support which I can at the present time. If you vote for me and I vote for me, we have the requisite two-thirds constitutional majority for replacement, and my own election, whereas I don't think you're capable of getting two-thirds support at the present time. There are certain weaknesses in your present position with which the opposition might disagree. A broad base of disagreement could be mounted against your candidacy and the move might well fall through."

"It might not if you would vote for me," I pointed out. "If I vote for me and you vote for me, that's the two-thirds majority again. And there would be a period of conciliation."

"Well," Davis said and shrugged, "you see that's the point. I mean, I find you perfectly viable and so on and

134

could work with you most equably should you be re-elected. But I must be responsible to my constituency and there is a great deal of dissatisfaction among certain elements. In all fairness, I would have to abstain on the question of your nomination. That would leave you 33⅓ percent short of the required majority."

"Well, if you won't do it for me, I don't see why I should do it for you. I'm not the only controversial figure here, you know. There is a great deal of opposition in *my* constituency to your own positions. I just don't think that you have the votes at the present time."

Davis shrugged uncomfortably, looked at the ceiling, down at his shoes and said, "Well, then, I gather that your position at the present time is flatly negative to my suggestion?"

"Not flatly negative. I think that the situation is wholly fluid. We should let things settle a bit."

"You don't agree with the seriousness?"

"Everything's serious," I said. "Nevertheless, I think that the best policy to follow in periods of flux is one of watchful waiting, patient, clearheaded, stoic observation followed by determined action when action is required. I do not see that action would be justified at the present time."

Without another word, Davis stood, unlocked the door and left my room. I do not know where he is at the present moment. Possibly he is conferring with Wilson again although I doubt it. That alliance seems to have been pretty well exhausted, something that I could have predicted from the outset, having seen this happen so many times before. It is indeed an extraordinary thing if Wilson himself wrecked the transmitters, but I suppose they will be fixed eventually, and in any event there had not been a message from Headquarters in several months prior to the difficulty, so it is not as if we are Losing Contact. Also, we have had little enough to say to Headquarters recently, other than that we are well and that the work on Ganymede, as always, continues.

HOW WE LIVE TODAY

As they have for a hundred years now, the life-support systems on Ganymede work well, and we are both insulated from and in total command of our environment. Here in this massive installation, several feet below the surface of the moon, we live in control of our machinery, carefully working out the measure of our development, kings of this moon as no Jovian ever was. If there ever were any Jovians. Finding out whether or not they exist or existed is one of the duties of this continuing project. We have several other duties, but the present political turmoil on Ganymede has made focussing on our tasks difficult.

THICKENING OF THE SITUATION, AN EMERGENCY IMPENDS

Today I received my second visit-in-quarters in less than a week—I am becoming more and more popular, it would seem—this time from Wilson who entered quickly with a furtive look on his face, and just as Davis, locked the door before joining me on my bunk. "I don't believe that he's following me," he said and we both understood that the *he* referred to Davis, "but one must be careful. I must talk to you about some very serious business."

"You couldn't call a session? You're aware of the rules on privacy, Mr. President, surely you can live with them."

During his tenure, a President is always referred to as *Mr. President* and in no other way, even in private conversations or correspondence. This is done in order to enforce that respect for the office and rule of law which is the key to the sustension of the colony on Ganymede.

"No," he said. "I could not. I am afraid that the

situation at the present time is absolutely perilous. I hate to tell you this, but the likelihood is that a full session would not be allowed to go through to completion. There are elements of sedition"—and he leaned forward to whisper this hoarsely—"elements of sedition, I must say, within the very councils of the government itself. It has come close. These are terrible times."

"Well," I said, "I don't quite know what to say. There's no reason to panic, however." Wilson had interrupted me while I was working on the stamp collection, and my mood had almost immediately turned poisonous. I have one of the largest and most impressive collections of Martian stamps available, and the job of collating and indexing, one which I undertook only recently, is nerve-wracking and demands the utmost concentration. "I think that a policy of watchful waiting remains the best bet. We can ride out the storm."

"You don't understand," Wilson said, leaning back to a slightly less precipitate position, his breath coming unevenly. "I have reason to believe that a coup is being planned. A coup against me. Against the duly constituted and legitimate Government of Ganymede."

"Led by whom?"

"By Davis. I've never liked him. I've understood from the start that he is dangerously ambitious. This could be held in check for a while, but I believe that he has panicked."

"We could use some reforms, you know," I said. "And it would help if the transmitter were set up again. Perhaps if we could communicate—"

"Listen," Wilson said, shaking his head, passing right over that, "I need your support. That's the reason I come to you. Together I believe we can ride out this very difficult and costly period. Separately—"

"What can I do?" I said. "The next election is coming along, at that time we can work something out. A change of administrations may solve the problem."

"There will be no next election. I have definite information that the seditionists will not permit elections to proceed peacefully. Terrorism, riots, sabotage, the wreck-

137

ing of equipment. Accordingly, I will find it necessary to declare martial law for the duration of the emergency. There can be no elections at this time."

It occurred to me then, not entirely for the first time, that Wilson was insane. He has evinced instability from the first, a certain unwillingness to accept the true facts of the situation, the reality of our mission on Ganymede, the obligations of our tour of duty. For a long time I put this down to nothing more than whimsy: there are certain bizarre aspects to the mission and a humorous man might seem to overemphasize them. What I had not understood was that Wilson on Ganymede was unable to duplicate his responses to stress situations on Earth. This is not the first time that such mistakes have been made, although on this project they have happily been kept to a minimum.

"Expulsion," he said. "Davis must be expelled from the councils and from the state. It is the only way. The traitor must be turned loose. He must be cleansed. Otherwise—"

"We need a unanimous vote for expulsion," I said. "You know that perfectly well. The full council must meet in extraordinary session and approve without dissenting vote."

"Not necessary," Wilson said and leaned toward me again with a mad, merry giggle. "Not necessarily. I have read the constitution, the statutes and the procedures carefully. There is a way."

"Not for unanimity. Unless you feel that Davis would vote for his own expulsion."

"Oh no. Certainly not. It would be contrary to the nature of the sedition-bastard to act in any other fashion than his own self-interest. No, I understand that part perfectly well. A technicality! A loophole!"

Only at this point did I put away the stamp collection, folding it into its exotic binders carefully, putting it into its place in the cabinets with that kind of cherishing skill which was the subject of a long profile-biography in *Philatelic Duo* three and a half years ago, when I had been first selected for the Ganymede Project. "The philatelic astronaut" was the subhead on the article and for a while I was embittered because I thought that I had been selected as *stamp's man of the decade* only because of the superficial publicity which could be generated by the fact that I was in the Program, but as the managing editor explained to me a few months later, it had not been like that at all: I had, after all, been well-known and respected as a stamp-collector long before I had become part of the Project, and it was not as an astronaut that I was being celebrated but rather a stamp-collector who had Done Something Useful. It was with a feeling of no small nostalgia that I put the precious collection away; since the failure of the transmitter I have been deprived of not only routine communication with Earth but that special twice-weekly call into my dealer inquiring as to new acquisitions, which had been one of the few high-points of the tour. "All right," I said, turning back to Wilson, who had turned virtually choleric in the interval and was now pacing back and forth in the cabin as if it was the hallway of a spaceship, "what's the loophole?"

"Well, let me tell you now," he said, "let me tell you, but I wish that you'd take more of an interest in things and try to concentrate; this stamp-collecting business of yours is fine and dandy in normal times, but when we are in a crisis, when things are virtually crumbling around us, it might be time for a little more reality, wouldn't you think? I mean, you've got to be reasonable about these things, I need your support very badly, but that doesn't mean that you've got an excuse to abuse the rigors of the office."

"I'm truly sorry, Mr. President," I said. The thing to do when Wilson becomes excitable is to humor him, a technique I learned early on. "I simply wanted to pay fullest attention to your suggestion and thus dispose of distracting influences."

"Ah," he said, "uh, ah, well, I understand this, but nevertheless in the future I wish you could concentrate a little *more*, well, under the provision of the Constitution, if a member of the duly constituted government becomes incompetent, that is to say that if he is unable to discharge his duties responsibly by reason of illness, insanity or death, then he can be excluded from the councils of the Government by a unanimous vote of the other duly elected representatives. Excluded, do you follow that? The judgment of incompetence is to be made in solemn plenary session to be summoned at the pleasure of the President. If the given representative is ruled incompetent, he may no longer participate in any of the functions of the state, he is confined to his quarters until such time as duly satisfactory relief is obtained, and he may not communicate to Headquarters other than through legislative fiat."

"You mean that you and I should vote that Davis is incompetent, is that what you're saying?"

Wilson nodded and said, "That's exactly it. This is a solemn plenary session which I have called. The President may call sessions when and where he chooses, at his own option, so that part is all right."

"So we should vote him incompetent? And then what?"

Wilson shrugged and fixed me with his curiously luminous gaze, a curiously unPresidential stare, no dignity or sense of removal in it whatsoever; the fact is that Wilson understands very little about the rigors of Administration and cannot even put on a good ceremonial front. His administrations have, consequently, lacked any kind of the pomp or high dignity which have characterized the others. "Well you see," he said, "they have that written up too in the Constitution: once a representative is determined incompetent, the disposition of that representative may be determined by the President. The President contacts Headquarters to advise them of the problem, and then while Headquarters is working on the relief, the President does all that he has to do in order to preserve order. To preserve order. So that's my option."

"I see," I said, and I did. "Nevertheless, if this vote went through, what would you do with Davis?"

"Well," Wilson said, "well, you see, under the circumstances, the sedition and everything, and the sabotage of the equipment and the breeding of revolution, supporting the violent overthrow of the Government and all that, why, that's treason. I mean, the crime is treason is what I have to say; how else can you look at it? So we'll have to kill him."

A GLIMPSE OF THE SURFACE:
STRANGE BEASTS DEPART

After the solemn plenary session, during the course of which a summary vote on the case of Davis was split one to one, no final judgment being arrived therefore on his incompetence at the present time (with another plenary session scheduled to be held soon, at some future date), after the President had left my quarters, after the sound of footsteps and murmuring in the corridors had subsided again to the whir of machines, after all of this I went alone into the planning room and from there used the periscope to look at the surface of the planet. Some day there may come beasts there, which is the only reason the equipment is maintained. In the periscope the surface is fading purple, colors of the spectrum at the edges washing toward that blandness; hint of rising gases in the mist, strange mineral forms and artifacts dotting the underlying rock. The full, gleaming sphere of Jupiter moves overhead, close as an apple, close to touch and on the surfaces of the planet, in my stress, I believe that I can see beasts walking: beasts as cannot be described, beasts beyond mythology; they are taking the surface of Ganymede in ponderous silence, their momentary bulk covering Jupiter, and when I wipe my eyes and return to the periscope, the beasts are gone; left only is the stone and gas of the moon itself, and I look upon it for a very long time, understanding that by being so deep in, we are not only beyond apprehension but beyond culpability; there is nothing that we can do to this moon or it to us; we can only bear it and bear it until our turn of duty is passed and then the others will come to do the same. If the present revolt will allow us to finish our turn of duty; it is difficult to say. After some time, I return to my quarters and fall into an uneasy sleep. It is difficult at this depth to feel that the seditionists are entirely wrong. There are things beyond here far more inimical than they.

THE GUTTING OF THE EQUIPMENT

During the night the revolutionaries struck. In the morning we confront disaster. The transmitter has been destroyed, the support systems wrecked, the hydroponics plant violated in a most disgusting manner. Only the emergency supplies and support remain, a margin which will carry us only through some fifty hours or far before the duly constituted elections and change of administration. Someone in the band has left notes in the corridors tacked up on walls saying: DEATH TO THE OPPRESSORS OF FREEDOM and WILSON EATS SHIT and POWER IS ETERNAL CORRUPTION; ONE MUST SMASH TO BE FREE and DIE EARTHMEN DIE and so on and so forth, the notes all the more disconcerting because they are beautifully calligraphed on fine paper and put up with the utmost care in careful symmetry. The destruction is monstrous, it proves that both Davis and Wilson were right, there is dangerous sedition in our midst. Perhaps my policy of watchful waiting was not the right one after all, but the true dimensions of the peril had evaded me until this moment. There is no question but that we must take very strong action now or face the dissolution of all those values which we have found to be the fundament of our lives.

THE END OF AN ADMINISTRATION

Wilson went out the dock in the afternoon, shortly after his discovery of the damage. I had been the first to see it but did not notify the others; feeling that it was best seen on our own and the individual responses assayed so that I could take proper action to detect that person or persons in the administration who were collaborating with the revolutionaries. "I can't stand it anymore!" Wilson said as Davis and I came from our rooms to stare at him, "didn't I tell you that the whole damned thing was insupportable? Think about it, think about it, the price they've made us pay!" and wrenched at the door so that he could get into the escape corridor. "We've got to take action, strong action now, or lose our freedoms forever!" he said, and the door came open. Davis leaned forward to tell Wilson that he did not have his equipment on and was thus undertaking certain death by entering the atmospheric contamination of the escape corridor, much less the elevator to the surface itself, but I restrained him with a sharp look, and in a moment he seemed to understand. Wilson, after all, remained the President and could not be contraindicted during the performance of his duties. "I tell you, I can't stand this anymore!" he said and stepped through the door, striding down the corridor. In a moment we could hear gasps and then the dull thump of the Presidential body hitting the floor, a few muffled shrieks and he was done for. Quickly Davis and I closed the door to maintain the integrity of the atmosphere. A little later we organized a recovery party and brought back the body of the dead President. He was buried in state that night, only the second occasion, other than the inaugurations, during which recordings of the full band were permitted to play. (I declared a state dinner as a gesture of respect to the Opposition during my third term, that was the only exception.) Later, Davis and I held an extraordinary session and martial law was declared. We are serving as a duly constituted military junta until the details of the next administration can be worked out; in the meantime, the junta has the full backing of the populace and is the duly constituted government. Our first project will be to clean out the seditionists, although their cowardly attacks have not been in evidence since this morning. Perhaps they are lying low.

A CONFERENCE AT THE SUMMIT

In bed, that night, I felt pain in sleep, and turning found that Davis had come in unclothed and without shoes, carrying a knife. He had stabbed me somewhere in an anterior area. I threw off sleep and came to my feet, we struggled murderously, and I succeeded in killing him by finding the pressure point over the jugular. He fell heavily, mumbling, and I instantly put the knife in safekeeping as evidence linking Davis to the crime. Then I checked his respiration and other gross signs to find that they were negative. With some regret I arranged for his disposition through the generator, this additional source of power extending the emergency ration for some four or five minutes, and then, without further ado, summoned an extraordinary session. There was nothing else to do.

"Gentlemen," I stated, "one faction of the junta by engaging in a vile and seditionist attempt to split the legitimate basis of power has brought things to a highly provocative state. Fortunately, the dissident elements have been removed, at great risk and with great cost. Nevertheless, it can now be said that for the first time since my last administration, a state of peace and tranquillity reigns. The revolutionaries have been crushed, their vile acts repudiated, their dreadful consequences cut off. A new era of peace and progress is about to begin." I then, without dissenting vote, declared an indefinite extension of martial law and named myself President with the power to hold off elections as long as necessary. Further extraordinary powers were granted. Options were granted. Certain leverages and permissions were granted. The government has been reconstituted around the new axis.

My first duty in my new role was to bring the transcripts of the Republic up to date, which has now been done. The transmitting equipment is quite hopeless so there is no way in which the situation can be relayed to Headquarters. This, however, will serve.

The locks click, feeding on Davis's body.

TOWARD A NEW ERA OF JUSTICE, KNOWLEDGE AND PEACE

All glints and hums in the silence now. Even on full, the machines will not supply power for more than an hour or so. I am afraid that the Republic is doomed. It has had a longer life than almost any of the other civilizations, but no less than any man is governed by rules of mortality, persistence, exchange and balancing action. It has had its great days, it has established its own monuments, now its time is done. Would that there be a fair judgment for the Republic which served its citizens so well. The skills of an historian are needed, are lacking in this situation.

Power all within and without; the hush of transmitter, gloom of Ganymede, wink of light. I have declared martial law and there is very little otherwise to do. I have guided the Republic safely to its destiny, and now, its last ruler—as was surely fated from the beginning—I wait out the final moments.

If the transmitter were reconstituted and I could talk to Headquarters again, could make one final statement in the void, I think I would say only this: "You bequeathed us a good system. You bequeathed us a good heritage. You gave unto us all of the gifts and grants of a grateful civilization. It is not your fault that it has come to this. You are not culpable. No matter how many times it has come to this, no matter how many times it will be repeated over and over again know that the fault is not with you. It is with the seditionists, with vile forms so low and cunning and directed that there is no way, with your basic decency or ours, that we can even confront them. Their methods are beyond us, their motives so unspeakably vile as to be beyond our control. This Moon contains the heart of the beast itself. There is no way we can conquer it. The revolution will always come and sweep us away.

"There is nothing we can do but to meet our fate with grace, with courage, and with that quiet acceptance so well summarized in the words of our late President who himself, before his untimely demise, saw the menace so clear and did as much as he could do to protect us."

The power is going out. I must conserve power and thus cease transcription. The Republic is in order. The Republic is at peace. At last duly constituted President of the Republic I look upon it and find it good because this Republic will survive, if not in our cells, then in the cells of so many individuals who in the generations to come, will reproduce it. The Republic will always be reconstituted afresh, anew. It is not its fault that it could not work on Ganymede. There is too much pain here.

Pain and loss beyond the possibility of grace. I wish I could save the stamps though. In a way it would all have been worth it if the Government had had the facilities to save the stamps. But they too will have to perish in the evacuation. Having triumphed over the dissidents, the Government is now going to demolish the project. This is necessary. Very little evidence after all must be left for the future revolutionaries prowling over the site. Very little evidence. Hark, hark! Blow the whole thing.

INTERVIEW WITH AN
ASTRONAUT, 2008

I had to climb five flights to get to the bastard. It was hell, believe me. There's nothing funny about these old-line tenements, particularly the carpeting they have on the stairs. It's at least half a century old and it's slippery. Of course the carpeting was never meant to be used or the staircases to be seen. But now that the elevators are out you can kill yourself. Not to complain, however. Every job has its drawbacks. Overall, I'm quite grateful.

I knocked at his door several times and heard mumblings and complaints inside. The usual routine; they hate to get out of bed. Once they're out of bed their problems begin. After a while I turned the knocks into real bangs and added a few curses. There's no sense in being kind to them. You have to let them know from the beginning who has the upper hand or they'll just take everything from you.

It worked. The door opened about wide enough to accommodate head and shoulders. He was a small man, alert bright eyes, a little bit younger looking than I would have figured from looking at the background statement. "What do you want?" he said. Sullen. Cautious. Confused. Hostile. The whole business. That pattern never changes.

I showed him my black pad in one hand, the identification card in the other. "Welfare," I said. "We're here to investigate that application of yours."

"I only filed yesterday. I thought it was supposed to take a week before they actually got someone out."

"There's a whole new procedure. We're trying to catch up on our pending applications, move a little bit ahead." That wasn't strictly true; the truth was that his application had interested me the moment the supervisor had put it on my desk. Even on my caseload, he was something out of the ordinary. But not unprecedented. Not unprecedented at all. There are ten of the bastards at least on relief right here in this city.

"All right, come in," he said and opened the door. So I went in.

The apartment was foul. Absolutely foul. It is impossible to convey how these people live. Litter in every corner, newspapers, smudges of food on the walls. That kind of thing. Inexcusable.

He saw me looking at it. "I'm demoralized," he said. "I don't feel so good. Things generally seem to be out of hand for me right now. All those newspapers, they're old, they're from the 1980's even. They mean something to me, I can't really explain it."

Big deal. I nodded at that bit of analysis, opened my book, and very cautiously edged to the center of the room to take the interview. You never sit down where these people have sat. And you have to watch out all the time for rats and insects. That's part of the training.

"Want to ask you a few questions," I said. "First—name, address and so on, all as verified on the application, right? John Steiner, 59 years old, this address. Yes?"

"You have all that. I gave all that in yesterday. I was waiting for the interview six hours and then they took it."

"But we have to make sure it's the same person," I explained. "Sometimes they send someone down for them, create a whole fictitious background, open up three or four cases all over the city. Once I had a bitch who was collecting it in *North Dakota* too. Flew in twice a week to keep the residence. We've got to protect the public." Before he could think about it, I took out my thumbprint kit, opened it, took his wrist, and pressed his thumb into the ink, then took the smudge on the paper inside and put the whole thing away. "Procedure," I said, "it's got to be done."

"It's just like the Program," he said. "I haven't felt more at home in years, you see. Total depersonalization of the individual, that's what it is. Don't you have enough regard to tell me what you're going to do first?"

"Some of them protest," I said. "They know they'll

148

get caught. Others start screaming about individual rights and so on. Hah! I'd like to tell you what *I* had to go through to get this job." I opened to his interview record and compared the physical description with him, it dovetailed reasonably well, considering the stupidity of the people who worked in intake. Most of them are there because something terrible happened to them in the field, you know, and they can't function anymore; the Department in its wisdom makes a place for them. "Just a few questions now," I said.

"Mind if I sit down?"

"You're ill? You can't stand. You need to rest?"

"Nothing like that," he said. "I just prefer to sit when I'm spoken to. It's an old courtesy."

"If you're sick enough we can probably get you into a fully reimbursed category. No difference to you but more money for us," I pointed out. "Did you pick up any plagues in space?"

"I'm not sick," he said again. "Just depressed. Not that that makes any difference to you people." The *you* rang out. One thing that can be counted on always, no matter where you go on the job, is this stolid hostility. If it were enjoyable, one would count it as a fringe benefit. I, as a matter of fact, do. It makes for a good working definition of the relationship. There is no hatred without fear and respect, two qualities which I like to command. And there is no way to overstate how I hate all these bastards. It was a pleasure, finally, to confront one. I intended to make it memorable for him.

He sat in an old chair in the center of the room. Moth-eaten cloth, intimations of small life crawling up and through the upholstery and so on. He lit a cigarette for me and tossed the match out the open window. Tinkle, splat.

"No," I said. "No cigarettes."

"What do you mean?"

"I don't like smoke," I said. "People don't smoke in my presence. At least, not people applying for relief. Put it out."

"No," he said. It was just like all the old transmissions you ever heard. The flat, dead, unyielding determination of the voice, the stultified tones. There was a difference, however. His eyes showed part of it and the other part was that he wasn't going nowhere. Nowhere.

"Throw it away," I said.

"I won't. I like to smoke. They never let you smoke on the Project and when I finally got to take it up I was hooked." The whine was coming back into his voice. "I know they're almost against the law but I don't care. They do me good."

"Fine," I said. "I'll do you more good by leaving. We'll call the whole thing *application withdrawn* on the records."

He looked at me for a moment. He could see I meant it. I'm very good at ultimatums, it's something you pick up early on in the job or otherwise you have no business being there at all. So after a time he threw the cigarette out the window, grumbling a trifle.

"Isn't that better?" I said.

"You really enjoy this, don't you? I mean, it gives you a certain kind of satisfaction, I can tell."

"Enjoy what?"

"This power. I used to be the same. I know what it's like. You can say things and *affect* people. I used to think that that was something really good, to be able to move people. Later on I understood what they were doing to us, but by then it was too late."

"Forget it," I said. "It's too late for any of that. I don't want your cheap analyses, you have nothing to say to me. Now I'll call it quits in one second if you don't cut it out."

Since he had lost the cigarette battle, this one wasn't even a skirmish. His eyes dropped.

"Occupational training?" I said.

"You *know* all that."

"Occupational training?"

"Astronaut," he said. Of course. "I went through all of that with your interviewer yesterday."

"I told you, I'm conducting my own investigation. I'm no rubber stamp, you'd better believe that I have the

150

power. The supervisor merely countersigns my work and as far as I'm concerned, you don't even exist until I say so. Why are you making application now?"

"Why do you think? I'm out of work."

"How did you support yourself prior to the application?"

He looked at me, almost pleading. "I went through all that," he said. "I told them and told them."

"The field investigator is the sole determinant of eligibility as he interprets the manual and regulations on public assistance. The intake unit passes on applications to the field investigator for exploration and judgment. You want any more quotes?"

"No," he said. I guess that is when I truly beat him. He seemed to cave in on the seat, his eyes turning inward, almost oblivious of the small things that seemed to be moving on his wrists. He had been easier to bring around than most of them; it was surprising in view of his credentials. But then again, everything considered, his credentials almost explained it.

They always did what they were told to do.

"I was with the Project for thirty years, ever since I took my master's degree. I was the twenty-ninth man on the moon, you know. When the Project ended six months ago, there were hundreds like me let go without any training or background for a single thing. And no one would hire me."

"No one would hire you," I said. "No one would hire you. Why wouldn't anyone hire the twenty-ninth man on the Moon?" *Twenty-ninth man on the Moon.* Would you believe that his voice cracked when he said that?

"Because they hate us," he said. "They all hate us."

That much was true.

"Why do they hate you?" I said. "Why do you seem to feel that there's all this hostility?"

He looked at me with perfect numbness and spread his hands. He said nothing, but it wasn't defiance, that had all been squeezed out. The point was that he had nothing to say. After a time he mumbled "Venus," and it sounded like a curse. "Venus."

"Venus?"

"How much do you want out of me? What do you want me to say? When I got into the Project, it was the thing to do. It was the salvation of the world and looked like it would be the most important thing by the end of the century. I made the wrong judgment! A lot of us made the wrong judgment! Was it our mistake? You probably weren't even born when all of this happened."

"Fortunately."

"They hate us," he said again. He seemed to like it. "They think that they can blame us for what happened. It had nothing to do with us at all. We were just used. Most of us knew it after a time, but it didn't matter. What else could we do? Who wanted us? And we thought that the end justified the means. The planets. The Centauris. Going out there. If you want to do something useful you have to put up with shit, that was the philosophy. End justifying the means, paying the price, taking the heat. We had nothing to do with it at all. But we're the ones who they can see so they hate us."

"Have you made efforts to seek other employment?"

"I've been everywhere. I have no skills that can be used and I've been nowhere. And they hate us."

"Yes, I gather that they hate you. You mean to say that there's no company who would hire the twenty-ninth man on the Moon, just for public relations?"

He gave me a sick grin and opened his palms flat. "Do you know what happened to the man who was first?" he said. "Do you know where the twenty-third and twenty-sixth are now? The eighth? The eleventh? Do you know what the fourteenth did to himself last week? I keep up. It's my only amusement now that I have no money for the races."

"In tough, huh?"

"Yes," said Steiner, "they're in tough."

Well, score one for him. At least he was being reasonable about the matter; he had accepted his position, he wasn't trying to push things. *He* knew where he stood; where the bodies were buried. It is surprising to gather, even at this date, how many of them refuse to admit it. I could have done anything I wanted to him then. Buggered him. Spat in his face. Or told him I was sorry that the Moon had turned out to be such bullshit. Being a professional, I did none of these things, being rather more interested in finding my personal pleasures elsewhere.

"So now you want assistance?" I said. "Public assistance. Relief. A handout for the troops."

"Do you see any alternative?" he said. His voice moved up on the *any* a little. Oh, he was sweating now: no doubt about it. Aside from certain bizarre occupational overtones, it was a perfectly routine investigation. I was competent. I was in the groove. I was doing my stuff.

"There should be *something*," I said. "How about a little unskilled labor?"

"They hate us," he said. "Do you understand that? *They hate us.*"

"I heard," I said drily, and with a little smile, just to show him that underneath this grim role occupied, I was a human being just as he was. "How about relatives? Any relatives who might furnish support?"

"My parents are dead. I don't know where my sister is, and I don't want to find her."

"That's not a legally responsible relative anyway."

"All right. I don't know where my ex-wife is either."

"You were married?"

"I put down all that yesterday."

"I told you, there are no yesterdays with us. We start from the beginning and we make our own history. When were you married?"

"1980. I haven't seen her since 1987. I think that she left the country, otherwise the computer would have turned her up. I did check her out a few months ago. No record."

"Why did she leave the country?"

"How would I know?"

"She didn't like the Project?"

He smiled at me and clasped his hands, wrung them slowly, palm to palm, and then dropped them on the chair. "No," he said, "she didn't like the Project. Most of the wives didn't, but she was one of those who came out and said it. She was—uh—difficult. It just couldn't be worked out."

"Why didn't she like it?"

"She said that the Project was constructed so that you had to buy everything, and she couldn't buy it anymore. Or try to sell it to people. Maybe it was the strain that got to her. It all got terribly involved, and when I was on the Moon flight, they had to hold her incommunicado. After that, it was just a question of calling it quits. It couldn't be. And I thought that the Project was going to go on forever, you see, so that if she couldn't adjust to it, it was her problem, I would always have something. I had no sense of the future," he said. "None at all. That was my problem, I never looked beyond what was going on. That was the way they taught us to think, and it was good for them. It was good for us, too, until all those things began happening."

Well, he had his point. A lot of us thought that the Project was going to go on forever, that it was just one of those timeless things. But we found out differently. There is nothing so large that it cannot be exposed and controlled. This is one of the blessings of understanding how things work.

"I guess that's about it," I said. "We'll keep you posted as things go on progressing; can't say exactly when, though."

"You mean I'm eligible?"

"I mean, I've completed the pending investigation now. Now, I have to go back and write it up—after I see a whole lot of other people; you know, you aren't the only case I've got; I've got a lot of obligations—and make my decision. Which I shall. Then you'll be notified."

"But listen," he said, gesturing toward me, "don't you understand? I have no money. I have no food. I got this place last week by telling the landlord that I'd be getting relief soon. I owe rent. I can't even turn around now, I tell you I can't operate!"

"You'll have to wait your turn. That's the way we do things down here on Earth, astronaut."

"But I haven't had a thing for three days—"

"You have running water," I said, pointing to the rusted tap in the corner suspended over a bucket. "That fills up the stomach pretty good in a bind. You'll hold, they got you in pretty good physical shape and you couldn't have lost it all so fast, even at your age." Then, because I really didn't want to smash him down all the way—the thing was to save him, build him up a little and know that you could do it to him an unlimited number of times in the future, I added, "You see, there are a lot of people I've got to service. You have to wait your turn. It's nothing personal, but the need is general. There's a lot of pain and deprivation in this city, a lot of funds were tied up for a long time, you know."

"Yes," he said, nodding. "The need is general. But don't blame the Project. We only tried to help it."

Crap. "I'm just trying to do a job, you understand. The job has to be done in a certain way."

"You've got a job," he said with some bitterness. "That's something to say, isn't it?"

"You know how much, how often, I think that I'd like to collect and let the people like you do this work? It's no picnic, believe me. The responsibility and the pressure. Not that anybody owes me any favors, you understand. But it's a tough racket. I work ten hours a day."

"I bet you love it," he said.

"What was that?"

"I said, I guess it's very tough. I have sympathy for you."

"Much better," I said. The interview was over now and the fun was all drained out of it. I had taken him, I suppose, to the best limits I could without breaking down the situation entirely and spilling everything.

I closed my book, put away the pencil, went to the door. "Any questions?" I asked.

"Why do they hate us?" he said, not looking at me. "Just that. Why? I understand that they do now and it took me a long time to face it, but I still don't know why."

"Think about it," I said. My last perception of him was a good one: staring stricken at the closing crack in the door. A hand moved idly to his face, dreamily, seemingly flyward, and I snapped off the image before it fumbled to his eyes and began scratching.

I went down the stairs three at a time.

In the street, I tossed my fieldbook and kit into the glove compartment of the car parked outside and then went down the way to have a beer before I went on to see the other bastards. I was scheduled to see three addicts and a whore that afternoon, but none of them would be in his class, that was for sure.

I went to a place named Joe's, which I had often visited before. Full of relief clients, of course. The bartender had common respect and was well-trained; he hopped to and kept them coming, and I kept the money away. He never asked for a cent. One of the bastards, trying to butter me up, asked how the job was going and what I was up to, and I said that I had just come from an interview with an astronaut and I thought I was going to turn the fucker down. "Good," said the reliefer, and started to tell the others, all up and down the bar, and then they were clapping and the singing and the laughing began, and all the afternoon I whiled away there in Joe's, feeling good and cheerful, screw the rest of the day, and when I went home it was with a full heart and a clean conscience: looking forward with high, bright anticipation to what I was going to do with that application when I got back to the office tomorrow.

RETURN TO THE MOON, 2311

It is not as if he had thought it would be. The domes push up into the stillness with no hint of erosion or age; the few artifacts that are on the surface seem to be new. He should have understood, of course, that the Moon has no atmosphere and thus is not subject to the normal slow ravages of time. (The trouble is that he actually thinks that way.) Still, he had expected something spectacular: ruination, perhaps, the picture of the Dome sunken into its own traces, corpses exuded from the surface, lying flat and bare to the sunlight. Nothing like this. This is how it must have been when it started. Of course the only difference is that there are no people now.

He is standing by the small ship, on the rim of a crater. He knows that he is perfectly safe, has an extended supply of support materials, and can wander over the Moon for hours after setting the beam on the ship for placement, but for some reasons he cannot fully understand, he finds himself reluctant to leave the site of the crater itself. Perhaps it is simple fear; perhaps it is something more profound. He feels rooted.

He had not known that it would be this way when he planned to make the voyage. Then he envisioned himself, somehow, running free on the Moon, the only living possibility within all these thousands of miles and somehow this experience would not only be a confirmation of his own existence—he has had trouble with this in the past—but a justification of it; surely no man who had travelled all this distance to be the only life on the Moon could have existed in vain. Indeed, he would have used the radio to transcribe his impressions and filter them back to the station; impressing anybody at the monitor with his coolness and poise, that quiet sense of destiny with which he was able to meet the unspeakable. But now he finds that he cannot do it. He cannot move from the ship. Indeed, as he looks at the surfaces of the moon, as he adjusts the filter on his helmet against the glare, he finds himself seized by nothing so much as an urge to return immediately to the ship and abandon the project right now. It is nothing personal. It has to do only with the sensations as he looks at the surface of the Moon. He had not reckoned on anything like this.

The transmitter in his suit clicks on, it is time for a routine check. "Everything all right there?" a voice asks. "Respond if correct." That is part of the service given by the bureau; the special feature of routine checks at stated intervals. It is one of their advantages over the competition although, as he has come to think of it during the trip, it makes little difference. What if he didn't respond? What if he got into trouble on the Moon? What if he became ill or some equipment malfunctioned? It is not as if they would be able to send someone to rescue him. That is another feature altogether and one which he could not have afforded. The package he has taken is the economy trip.

"All right," he says.

"Any problems with suiting, instruments, so on?"

"No," he says. "Everything looks clear."

"Good," says the voice, "very good. We'll check with you again in two hours then. Good luck." And it clicks off before he is given a chance to tell them of his psychological stage. He had been ready to tell them exactly how he felt at this moment and of the quality of his feelings. Of course that is not included in the package; he has not requested constant-monitor. That comes into an entirely different category and just as his parents could not have afforded the rescue-option, they could not manage the monitor. He does not blame them. They have done the best that they could, and the important thing is that they have given him what they had promised: a trip to the Moon as a graduation present. He has no quarrel with them, not on this score anyway. As far as the other things, they hardly matter any more. He is 22 years old. He has learned to accept reality.

He hovers at the brink of the crater again, telling himself that there is nothing to it: really nothing at all, it is only a question of putting one foot in front of the next, over and out, into the rocks and over to the Dome itself, where he can use any one of the portholes to go inside. He can look around in the receiving part of the Dome for a while and then go back to the ship and get out of there. There is no menace to it and it is not as if there is anyone alive here. But again he cannot make himself do it. He admits to himself that he is afraid, and the sense of calculation and insight that this gives him is almost a kind of power in itself, but it does not aid him in leaving the crater. After a time, he says *the hell with it* and goes back to the ship.

Inside the ship he sits for a time, thinking of very little at all, idly playing with the absorptive-blocks which, along with his music tapes, had occupied him on the voyage outward, and humming to himself. He has removed his suit which hangs in parody of his own figure against one of the walls and in the position which he has put it, one arm extended, it seems to grossly beckon, a suggestion which takes on heightened meaning in the close quarters. He is not unaware of the symbolism of this: part of him—the outer part, the superficial part—is telling him to go outside on the Moon, but that interior section, that place in which he lives and will have to live for a long time to come. . . . that section will not permit him. So he sits and toys with the blocks and waits for the next monitor transmission. He figures that if he can stay on the surface for three or four hours, he will have covered himself, and no one will ever have to know—unless he tells them, and this will always be his option. He can decide. When he gets married, perhaps, he will tell his wife on their wedding night.

"I went to the Moon," he imagines himself saying, "went to the Moon on one of those individual fly-it-yourself deals for graduation, something that I had looked forward to all my life, and do you know something? When I got there, I found that I didn't want to go anywhere on it. That there was nowhere to go. That I was afraid to

159

move from the crater, that I did not want to see the Dome. And so I stayed there for a few hours, alone in the craft, waiting the time out, and then I returned and told everyone that I had conquered the Moon. And they thought that that was very nice. Do you understand what I'm saying?"

And the girl he will marry—the kind of girl he has always known he will marry, the only kind of girl for him—this girl will turn toward him then in the strange light of the room, the first room of their joining, and she will toss her hair back from her head, running a palm across her brow, her eyes alight for him, and she will say, "Well of course. Of course. What is there to worry about? What does the Moon matter? And why must the measure of a man be what he does on the Moon?" And everything will be fine then, everything will be right between them and they will make love all night, the surfaces of one moving against the other, touching and brushing in the husk of the night, and at the end of the night will come a vision and the vision will be something so profound, so meaningful, so utterly central to him that it will vault to the inside, he leaping to absorb it, and this vision, this knowledge, this insight, he knows, will irrevocably change his life.

April, 1970
New York, New York